Kate Hoffmann's Mighty Quinns are back—and this time, they're going Down Under!

All Quinn males, past and present, know the legend of the first Mighty Quinn. And they've all been warned about the family curse—that the only thing capable of bringing down a Quinn is a woman.

These sexy Aussie brothers are about to learn that they can't escape their family legacy, no matter where they live. And they're about to enjoy every satisfying minute of it!

Watch for:

THE MIGHTY QUINNS: BRODY
June 2009

THE MIGHTY QUINNS: TEAGUE
July 2009

THE MIGHTY QUINNS: CALLUM
August 2009

Dear Reader,

Can you believe it? The Quinns are back! These boys just won't let me get a moment's rest. But this time I've put a bit of twist to the story. I've set this new trilogy "down under." These three Quinn brothers are Irish-Australian. But they're as sexy as their American cousins.

Setting the story in Australia seemed like such a simple task in the proposal stage. But as I began to write the books, I found out how much I didn't know about the country. My research turned into a travelogue of sorts, and now I'm definitely going to have to save my pennies for a trip there.

Brody is the youngest Quinn brother in this trilogy and he is a heartbreaker. But he meets his match in an American girl, Payton Harwell, an heiress who just wants to lose herself in the vastness that is Australia—while she loses herself in Brody's arms.

I hope you enjoy the new Quinn trilogy. And don't worry. These probably won't be the last Quinn books. I'm growing very fond of these boys!

Happy reading,

Kate Hoffmann

Kate Hoffmann

THE MIGHTY QUINNS: BRODY

TORONTO • NEW YORK • LONDON
AMSTERDAM • PARIS • SYDNEY • HAMBURG
STOCKHOLM • ATHENS • TOKYO • MILAN • MADRID
PRAGUE • WARSAW • BUDAPEST • AUCKLAND

Recycling programs
for this product may
not exist in your area.

ISBN-13: 978-0-373-79480-5

THE MIGHTY QUINNS: BRODY

www.eHarlequin.com

Printed in U.S.A.

ABOUT THE AUTHOR

Kate Hoffmann has been writing for Harlequin Books for fifteen years and has published nearly sixty books, including Harlequin Temptation novels, Harlequin Blaze books, novellas and even the occasional historical. When she isn't writing, she is involved in various musical and theatrical activities in her small Wisconsin community. She enjoys sleeping late, drinking coffee and eating bonbons. She lives with her two cats, Tally and Chloe, and her computer, which shall remain nameless.

Books by Kate Hoffmann

Don't miss any of our special offers. Write to us at the following address for information on our newest releases.

Harlequin Reader Service
U.S.: 3010 Walden Ave., P.O. Box 1325, Buffalo, NY 14269
Canadian: P.O. Box 609, Fort Erie, Ont. L2A 5X3

For Sarah Mayberry, fellow author and gentle reader, who took the time to make sure this book had "no worries."

Prologue

Queensland, Australia—January, 1994

"HOW CAN A ROCK be magic?" Callum asked, standing at the base of the huge boulder. "It's just a bloody big rock."

"Look around you, dipstick," Teague shouted from the top of the rock. "Do you see any other rocks like this around here? Gramps said it's here because it *is* magic. You stand on top of this rock and make a wish and it comes true. Aborigines brought it here and they know a lot of magic."

"I think Gramps had a few kangaroos loose in the paddock." Callum chuckled. "I wouldn't believe everything he said."

Brody stepped up to the rock. "He did not. And I'm telling Dad you said that. It's not nice to speak ill of the dead."

"He told us there was treasure buried out here, too," Callum said. "He even told me he dug for it when he was a boy. Who would bury treasure out here?"

Brody punched Callum in the shoulder. "Give me a leg up," he said.

"No, we have to get back. Mum will have supper ready."

"I want to climb it," Brody insisted. It was hard enough always being last in line, but he hated it when Callum tried to be the boss. At least Teague liked to explore and have adventures. He treated Brody as if they were the very same age, not eighteen months apart. Callum was always the careful one, warning them off when things got too dangerous. Three years older than Brody and he might have well been forty, Brody thought.

"You'll fall and crack your noggin open," Callum warned. "And I'll get the blame, just like I always get the blame for every bad thing you morons do."

"Cal, help him up," Teague said. "It's not that high. And I'll hang on to him."

"You don't have to hang on to me," Brody said. "I'm not a baby."

Reluctantly, Callum wove his fingers together and bent down. Brody put his foot into his older brother's hands and a few moments later, Teague had dragged him to the top of the rock. "Wow," Brody said. "This is high. I bet I can see all of Queensland from here."

"You've climbed to the top of the windmills. They're much higher," Callum said as he scrambled up behind him. "And you can't see Brisbane from them. And Brisbane *is* in Queensland."

"Make a wish," Teague said. "We'll see if it works."

"I have to think," Brody said. He wanted so many things. A computer, video games, a dirt bike. But there was something he wanted more than anything. He'd never told his brothers because he knew they'd laugh. After all, there wasn't much chance he'd ever get off the station.

"Come on," Teague said. "Say it. It won't come true unless you shout it out loud."

"I want to be a footballer," Brody yelled. "I want to go to a real school and play on a real team. I want to be famous and everyone will know my name. And I want to be on the telly." To Brody's surprise, his brothers didn't laugh. In fact, they seemed to think his wish was a good one.

"That's a big wish," Callum said soberly.

"My turn," Teague said. "I know exactly what I want. I want an airplane. Or a helicopter. I want to learn how to fly. Then I can go anywhere I want, just like that. I could even fly over the ocean and see America or Africa or the South Pole."

"You could take me to my football games," Brody said.

Teague reached out and ruffled Brody's hair. "I could. But only if you give me free tickets." He stared over at Callum. "What about you?"

"I know what I want," Callum said.

"You have to say it."

Callum sat down, draping his arms over his knees as he took in the view. "How do you think this rock really got here?"

"I think it's a meteor," Brody said, sitting down beside him. "It dropped out of the sky."

Callum ran his hand over the smooth surface of the rock. "Maybe the Aborigines did move it here. Maybe it was like Stonehenge. You know, that place in England with all the rocks."

"And I think a giant prehistoric bird took a crap and it fossilized," Teague teased as he joined them. They all laughed, lying back on the rock and staring up at the cloudless sky.

Brody wrinkled his nose. "How can bird poop be magic, Teague?"

"Maybe it came from a magic bird." His brother gave him a sideways glance. "All right. It's a meteor. Or an asteroid. From another universe. Come on, Cal, you have to make your wish now."

Callum drew a deep breath. "I wish that someday I could have a place like this."

"You want a rock?" Brody asked.

"No, dickhead. A station. As big as Kerry Creek. Bigger, even. And I'd raise the best cattle in all of Queensland."

"Why would you want to live on a station?" Brody asked.

"'Cause I like it here," Callum replied.

Brody shook his head. His older brother had no imagination. Station life was horribly dull, the same thing day after day. There was never anything interesting to do. All the good stuff happened in cities like Brisbane and Sydney. Callum could have the station and Teague could have his plane. Brody knew his dream was the best.

"Dad told me he brought Mum out here when he asked her to marry him," Callum said, sitting up to scan the horizon.

Teague and Brody glanced at each other, then looked away silently. Brody wasn't sure why Callum had brought the subject up. Their parents hadn't been getting along for nearly a year now. When they weren't arguing, they were avoiding each other. Dinner was usually a shouting match or an endless meal marked by dead silence.

"I want to change my wish," Brody murmured,

sitting up beside Callum. "I wish that Mum and Dad wouldn't fight anymore. I wish they'd be like they used to be." He drew a deep breath, fighting back the tears that pressed at the corners of his eyes. "Remember when they used to kiss? When Dad would hug her so hard, she'd laugh? And they'd turn on the radio and dance around the kitchen?"

"Yeah." Teague braced his elbows behind him. "I remember that."

The first ten years of Brody's life had been spent in what he'd believed was a happy family. But then he began to be more aware of his mother's unhappiness and of his father's frustration. She hated life on the station and his father didn't know any other life *but* the station.

Callum grabbed Brody's hand and then Teague's and pressed all their hands together. "Wish it," he said, dragging them closer. "Close your eyes and wish it really hard and it will happen."

"I thought you didn't believe in the rock," Teague said.

"Do it!" Callum said. "Now."

They all closed their eyes and focused on the one wish. But somehow, Brody knew this wish didn't depend on the rock or the combined powers of the three Quinn brothers. It was up to their parents to make it come true.

When he opened his eyes, he found his brothers staring at him. Brody forced a smile, but it did nothing to relieve his fears. Something bad was going to happen, he could feel it.

He rolled over onto his stomach and slid down the side of the rock, dropping to the dusty ground with a soft thud. His horse was tethered nearby and he grabbed the reins and swung up into the saddle. As he watched his brothers jump down, Brody couldn't help but wonder whether the rock had heard them. It was just a rock. And though it didn't belong where it was, there probably wasn't anything special about it.

Pulling hard on the reins, he kicked his horse in the flanks and took off at a gallop. If his mother left the station, then he was going with her. She'd need someone to take care of her, and Brody had always been able to make her smile. She'd once whispered to him that he was her favorite. If that was true, then it was his duty to leave the station. He felt the tears tumbling from his eyes and drying on his cheeks as the wind rushed by.

The breeze caught the brim of his stockman's hat and it flew off, the string catching around his neck. Brody closed his eyes and gave the horse control over their destination. Maybe the horse wouldn't go home. Maybe it would just keep galloping, running to a place where life wasn't quite so confusing.

1

Queensland, Australia—June, 2009

HIS BODY ACHED, from the throbbing in his head to the deep, dull pain in his knee. The various twinges in between—his back, his right elbow, the fingers of his left hand—felt worse than usual. Brody Quinn wondered if he'd always wake up with a reminder of the motorcycle accident that had ruined his future or, if someday, all the pain would magically be gone.

Hell, he'd just turned twenty-six and he felt like an old man. Reaching up, he rubbed his forehead, certain of only one thing—he'd spent the previous night sitting on his arse at the Spotted Dog getting himself drunk.

The sound of an Elvis Presley tune drifted through the air and Brody knew exactly where he'd slept it off— the Bilbarra jail. The town's police chief, Angus Embley, was a huge fan of Presley, willing to debate the King's singular place in the world of music with any bloke who dared to argue the point. Right now, Elvis was only exacerbating Brody's headache.

"Angus!" he shouted. "Can you turn down the music?"

Since he'd returned home to his family's cattle station in Queensland, he'd grown rather fond of the accommodations at the local jail. Though he usually ended up behind bars for some silly reason, it saved him the long drive home or sleeping it off in his SUV. "Angus!"

"He's not here. He went out to get some breakfast."

Brody rolled over to look into the adjoining cell, startled to hear a female voice. As he rubbed his bleary eyes, he focused on a slender woman standing just a few feet away, dressed in a pretty, flowered blouse and blue jeans. Her delicate fingers were wrapped around the bars that separated them, her dark eyes intently fixed on his.

"Christ," he muttered, flopping back onto the bed. Now he'd really hit bottom, Brody mused, throwing his arm over his eyes. Getting royally pissed was one thing, but hallucinating a female prisoner was another. He was still drunk.

He closed his eyes, but the image of her swirled in his brain. Odd that he'd conjured up this particular apparition. She didn't really fit his standard of beauty. He usually preferred blue-eyed blondes with large breasts and shapely backsides and long, long legs.

This woman was slim, with deep mahogany hair that fell in a riot of curls around her face and shoulders. By his calculations, she might come up to his chin at best. And her features were…odd. Her lips were almost too lush and her cheekbones too high. And her skin was so pale and perfect that he had to wonder if she ever spent a day in the sun.

"You don't have to be embarrassed. A lot of people talk in their sleep."

Brody sat up. She had an American accent. His fantasy women never had American accents. "What?"

She stared at him from across the cell. "It was mostly just mumbling. And some snoring. And you did mention someone named Nessa."

"Vanessa," he murmured, scanning her features again. She wasn't wearing a bit of makeup, yet she looked as if she'd just stepped out of the pages of one of those fashion magazines Vanessa always had on hand. She had that fresh-scrubbed, innocent, girl-next-door look about her. Natural. Clean. He wondered if she smelled as good as she looked.

Since returning home, there hadn't been a single woman who'd piqued his interest—until now. Though she could be anywhere between sixteen and thirty, Brody reckoned if she was younger than eighteen, she wouldn't be sitting in a jail cell. It was probably safe to lust after her.

"You definitely said Nessa," she insisted. "I remember. I thought it was an odd name."

"It's short for Vanessa. She's a model and that's what they call her." Nessa was so famous, she didn't need a last name, kind of like Madonna or Sting.

"She's your girlfriend?"

"Yes." He drew a sharp breath, then cleared his throat. "No. Ex-girlfriend."

"Sorry," she said with an apologetic shrug. "I didn't mean to stir up bad memories."

"No bad memories," Brody replied, noting the hint of defensiveness in his voice. What the hell did he care what this woman thought of him—or the girls he'd dated? He swung his legs off the edge of the bed, then raked his hands through his hair. "I know why *I'm* here. What are *you* doing in a cell?"

"Just a small misunderstanding," she said, forcing a smile.

"Angus doesn't lock people up for small misunderstandings," Brody countered, pushing to his feet. "Especially not women." He crossed to stand in front of her, wrapping his fingers around the bars just above hers. "What did you do?"

"Dine and dash," she said.

"What?"

Her eyes dropped and a pretty blush stained her cheeks. "I—I skipped out on my bill at the diner down the street. And a few other meals in a few other towns. I guess my life of crime finally caught up with me. The owner called the cops and I'm in here until I find a way to work it off."

He pressed his forehead into the bars, hoping the cool iron would soothe the ache in his head. "Why don't you just pay for what you ate?"

"I would have, but I didn't have any cash. I left an IOU. And I said I'd come back and pay as soon as I found work. I guess that wasn't good enough."

Brody let his hands slide down until he was touching her, if only to prove that she was real and that he wasn't dreaming. "What happened to all your money?" he asked, fixing his attention on her face as he ran his fingers over hers. It seemed natural to touch her, even though she was a complete stranger. Oddly, she didn't seem to mind.

Her breath caught and then she sighed. "It's all gone. Desperate times call for desperate measures. I'm not a dishonest person. I was just really, really hungry."

She had the most beautiful mouth he'd ever seen, her

lips soft and full…perfect for— He fought the urge to pull her closer and take a quick taste, just to see if she'd be…different. "What's your name?"

"Payton," she murmured.

"Payton," he repeated, leaning back to take in details of her body. "Is that your last name or your first?"

"Payton Harwell," she said.

"And you're American?"

"I am."

"And you're in jail," he said, stating the obvious.

She laughed softly and nodded as she glanced around. "It appears I am. At least for a while. Angus told me as soon as he finds a way for me to work off my debt, he'll let me out. I told him I could wash dishes at the diner, but the owner doesn't want me back there. I guess jobs are in short supply around here."

Brody's gaze drifted back to her face—he was oddly fascinated by her features. Had he seen her at a party or in a nightclub in Fremantle, he probably wouldn't have given her a second glance. But given time to appreciate her attributes, he couldn't seem to find a single flaw worth mentioning.

"Quinn!"

Brody glanced over his shoulder and watched as Angus strolled in, his freshly pressed uniform already rumpled after just a few hours of work. "Are you sober yet?"

"You didn't have to lock me up," Brody said, letting go of the bars.

"Brody Quinn, you started a brawl, you broke a mirror and you threw a bleedin' drink in my face, after insulting my taste in music. You didn't give me a choice." Angus braced his hands on his hips. "There'll be a fine. I figure a couple hundred should do it. And you're gonna have to pay for Buddy's mirror." Angus scratched his chin. "And I want a promise you're gonna behave yourself from now on and respect the law. Your brother's here, so pay the fine and you can go."

"Teague is here?" Brody asked.

"No, Callum is waiting. He's not so chuffed he had to make a trip into town."

"I could have driven myself home," Brody said.

"Your buddy Billy tried to take your keys last night. That's what started the fight. He flushed the keys, so Callum brought your spare." Angus reached down and unlocked the cell. "Next time you kick up a stink, I'm holding you for a week. That's a promise."

Brody turned back and looked at Payton. "You can let her out. I'll pay her fine, too."

"First you have to settle up with Miss Shelly over at the coffeeshop and then you have to find this young lady a job. Then, I'll let you pay her fine. Until you do all that, she's gonna be a guest for a bit longer."

"It's all right," Payton said in a cheerful voice. "I'm okay here. I've got a nice place to sleep and regular meals."

Brody frowned as he shook his head. It just didn't feel right leaving her locked up, even if she did want to stay. "Suit yourself," he said, rubbing at the ache in his head.

Payton gave him a little wave, but it didn't ease his qualms. Who was she? And what had brought her to Bilbarra? There were a lot of questions running through his mind without any reasonable answers.

He walked with Angus through the front office

toward the door. "Let her out, Angus," he said in a low voice. "I'll fix any mess she's made."

"I think she wants to stay for a while. I'm not sure she has anywhere else to go. I figure, I'll find her a job and at least she'll eat." He cleared his throat. "Besides, she doesn't complain about my music. She actually likes Elvis. Smart girl."

When they reached the front porch of the police station, Brody found his eldest brother, Callum, sitting in an old wooden chair, his feet propped up on the porch railing, his felt stockman's hat pulled low over his eyes.

Brody sat down next to him, bracing his elbows on his knees. "Go ahead. Get it over with. Chuck a spaz and we'll call it a day."

Callum shoved his hat back and glanced at his little brother. "Jaysus, Brody, this is the third time this month. You keep this up, you might as well live here and save yourself the trouble driving the two hours into town every weekend. At least I wouldn't worry about how you're getting home."

"It won't happen again," Brody mumbled.

"I can't spare the time. And petrol doesn't come cheap. And it's not like I don't have enough on my mind with this whole land mess boiling up again."

Callum had been a grouch for the past month, ever since Harry Fraser had filed papers in court to contest what had to be the longest-running land dispute in the history of Australia. Harry ran the neighboring station and the Frasers and the Quinns had been feuding for close to a hundred years, mostly over a strip of land that lay between the stations—land with the most productive water bore within a couple hundred kilometers.

Ownership of the property had passed back and forth over the years, dependant on the judge who heard the case. It was now the Quinns' property to lose.

"He's lost the last three times he tried. He hasn't been able to find any decent proof of his claim. What makes you think that will change now?"

"I'm still going to have to hire a bloody solicitor and they don't come cheap." Callum sighed. "And then this genealogy woman just shows up on the doorstep yesterday morning and expects me to spend all my time telling stories about our family history."

"I said I was sorry."

"You're turning into a fair wanker, you are. You could find something better to do with yourself. Like lending a hand on the station. We could use your help mustering now that Teague's practice is starting to take off. He's been taking calls almost every day. And when he's home, he spends his time doing paperwork."

"I haven't decided on a plan," Brody muttered. "But it bloody well doesn't include stockman's work. Now, can I have my keys? I've got some things to do."

"Buddy doesn't want you back at the Spotted Dog. You're going to have to find yourself another place to get pissed—" Callum paused "—or you could give up the coldies. It would save you some money."

Brody's brother Teague had been back on Kerry Creek for about a year after working as an equine vet near Brisbane. He'd taken up with Doc Daley's practice in Bilbarra, planning to buy him out so that the old man could retire. He'd saved enough in Brisbane to purchase a plane, making it possible to move about the outback quickly and efficiently.

Callum's income came directly from working Kerry Creek, the Quinn family's fifty-thousand-acre cattle station. Part of the profits went to their parents, now living in Sydney, where their mother taught school and their father had started a small landscaping business in his retirement.

And Brody, who'd once boasted a rather impressive bank account, was now unemployed, his million-dollar contract gone, many of his investments liquidated and his savings dwindling every day. He could survive another three or four years, if he lived frugally. But after that, he needed to find a decent job. Something that didn't involve kicking a football between two goalposts.

When Brody had left the station as a teenager, there'd been no other choice. He'd hated station life almost as much as his mother had. And though he'd wanted to stay with his brothers, his mother needed someone to go with her, to watch out for her. It had been a way to realize his dream of a pro-football career and he'd grabbed the chance. If it hadn't been for the accident, he'd still be living in Fremantle, enjoying his life and breaking every last scoring record for his team.

One stupid mistake and it had ended. He'd torn up his knee and spent the last year in rehab, trying to get back to form. He'd played in three games earlier in the season before the club dropped him. No new contract, no second chance, just a polite fare-thee-well.

"I'm sorry you're not doing what you want to do," Callum said, reaching out and putting his hand on Brody's shoulder. "Sometimes life is just crap. But you pick yourself up and you get on with it. And you stop being such a dickhead."

Brody gave his brother a shove, then stood up. "Give it a rest. If I needed a mother, I'd move back to Sydney and live with the one I already have." Brody grabbed his keys from Callum's hand then jogged down the front steps and out into the dusty street. "I'll catch you later."

As he walked down the main street of Bilbarra, his thoughts returned to the woman sitting in Angus's cell. "Payton," he whispered. He hadn't been attracted to any woman since Vanessa had walked out on him a year ago, frustrated by his dark moods and eager to find a bloke with a better future and a bigger bank account.

But Payton Harwell didn't know him, or football. All she cared about was a place to sleep and her next meal. And he certainly had the means to provide that.

PAYTON SIPPED at the bottle of orange juice that Angus had brought for her breakfast. She'd finished the egg sandwich first, then gobbled down the beans and bacon, enough nutrition to last her the entire day. Sooner or later, Angus would let her out and then she'd be back to scraping by for her meals. It was best to eat while she could.

She glanced over at the adjoining cell. It had been pleasant to have some company for a time, she mused. Actually, more than pleasant when the fellow prisoner was as handsome and fascinating as Brody Quinn. Payton rubbed the spot where their hands had touched, remembering the sensation that had raced through her at the contact.

She'd been in Australia for a month now and this had been the first real conversation she'd allowed herself.

She'd told him her name, but not much else. In truth, since her arrival, Payton had spent most of her time trying to figure out exactly who she was, now that she wasn't what she was supposed to be.

Until a month ago, her life had always been neatly laid out in front of her—the best schools, carefully chosen activities, the right friends, exotic vacations. As she grew older, a top-notch education and a careful search for an appropriate husband. Finally, a wonderful wedding to a successful man that her parents adored. It had been exactly the path her mother had followed, a step-by-step guide to happiness.

Payton had taken on the role of the dutiful daughter, doing all she could to please her parents and never once rebelling against their authority. Even when they'd insisted she stop riding at age seventeen after breaking her arm in a fall, Payton had agreed. She'd loved her horse, and riding had given her a wonderful sense of freedom. But she'd simply assumed that her parents knew best. If she'd had a rebellious streak, it hadn't shown itself—until a month ago. And then, it had erupted like a dormant volcano.

When it came to the moment to say "I do," Payton had turned and run. For the first time in her life, she'd made a decision for herself. Though she was twenty-five years old, her perfect life up to that point had never prepared her to deal with self-doubt. Running had been her only option.

She'd met Sam her first day at Columbia. He was the man her mother had always told her about, the man who could give her everything she'd ever want or need. He was handsome and smart, four years older, and from a wealthy

East Coast family. Her father, the scion of a banking empire, approved of his finances, and her mother, a third-generation socialite, approved of his bloodlines. And it wasn't as if there hadn't been an attraction between them. There had been…in the beginning.

An image flashed in her mind. How easily she'd forgotten Sam. All she wanted to think about now was this stranger who had touched her, this man with the penetrating gaze and the dangerous smile. A tiny thrill raced through her at the memory of his eyes raking the length of her body.

Payton leaned her head back against the concrete wall of the cell. Brody Quinn was incredibly sexy. Any woman would be attracted to a man like that. She allowed herself to speculate. Shirt on, shirt off. Completely naked and—without the bars between them, she wondered just how far she would have gone. A kiss, a quick grope, maybe more?

Payton sighed. Maybe her attraction to Brody wasn't an early midlife crisis. Maybe she was experiencing some sort of sexual schizophrenia caused by all the stress she'd been under. She'd never thought a whole lot about sex until recently. It had never been that important.

But suddenly, she found herself thinking about passion and desire, about what it truly meant to connect on a physical level with a man. Wasn't it normal for her to worry if Sam was the last man she'd ever sleep with? Shouldn't he want to touch her and make her moan with pleasure? Shouldn't sexual attraction be just as important as love and mutual respect?

There hadn't been that many men in her life—a grand total of four—so she hadn't much experience on which to rely. Two boys in high school, one in college after she and Sam had broken up for a time, and then Sam. She knew sex was supposed to be exciting and it had been, up until Sam had started working twelve- to fourteen-hour days. Suddenly, intimacy had become just another job for him, an obligation, like the bouquet of flowers he brought her every Friday evening.

In the weeks before the wedding, her mother had assured her it would all even out over time. There were meant to be highs and lows in a marriage. It kept things interesting. And heaven knows, she'd said, sex wasn't everything. She and Payton's father kept separate bedrooms and they got along just fine.

Until that moment, Payton had always assumed the arrangement was because her father snored, but once she realized her parents no longer needed each other in that way, she began to question her assumptions about a happy marriage. She wondered if her own marriage might end up more a convenient arrangement than a lifelong passion.

From that point on, Payton began to look at Sam in a different way. Every touch, every kiss, was more evidence that the passion between them was waning. Worse, she began to doubt herself. Perhaps she was just incapable of keeping a man sexually interested. Maybe it was genetic.

But that crazy attraction hadn't been missing with Brody Quinn. There had been an excitement between them, a delicious anticipation that she hadn't felt in a very long time. Her heart beat faster at the thought of him, and her breathing suddenly grew shallow. He'd been attracted to her, too, that much was obvious.

She thought back to the night before her wedding, a night spent pacing her room at the resort in Fiji. Every instinct told her to call it all off—or at least delay until she had her head on straight. But she knew what an embarrassment it would be to her parents, how upset they'd be. As an only child, so much had always been expected of her, and she'd done her best to make her parents proud. But wasn't there a point in life where she had to think about herself first?

It had taken her until the very last minute to decide to run. She'd been walking across the terrace on her father's arm, the ocean breezes ruffling her silk dress as family and friends waited on the beach. Her father had kissed her cheek and handed her over to Sam. Yet when she'd looked into Sam's eyes, Payton knew she couldn't go any further.

She tried to push the memory aside, taking another sip of orange juice as she fought back the tears that threatened. She'd run straight back to the room and grabbed her passport and a single bag. Five minutes later, she was on her way to the airport, still dressed in her white gown, ready to take the first flight off Fiji to anywhere in the world.

But a new charge on her credit card might betray her. So she'd exchanged her honeymoon ticket to Sydney for a ticket to Brisbane, assured that the airlines would keep her plans confidential. She had a visa, so it had been no problem entering the country. And once she was there, it had been even easier to lose herself.

Unfortunately, even following a strict budget, the cash she'd had with her had only gone so far. She'd heard from a woman in Brisbane that there were often jobs available for foreigners at some of the cattle and sheep stations in Queensland. They offered room and board and a decent wage—and for Payton, a place to hide out until she could bear facing her family again.

Perhaps it wouldn't be so difficult to go back, she mused. She could call her parents and explain the pressure she'd been under. Perhaps Sam might even forgive her. She drew a ragged breath. But would that stop these feelings of doubt?

Her mind flashed an image of Brody Quinn again and warmth snaked through her veins. He was dangerously handsome, his body lean and muscular, probably toned more by hard work than hours in the gym. His skin was burnished brown by the sun and his rumpled hair was streaked with blond.

But it was his eyes that she found fascinating. They were an odd color—part green, part gold—and ringed with impossibly long lashes. He didn't say much, but when he spoke, she found his accent entirely too charming. And when he looked at her, she had to wonder what he was thinking. Had he been undressing her in his head? Had he been thinking about more than just touching and kissing?

Had Angus not let him out, Payton wondered whether they might have acted on the attraction. In truth, he'd made her feel something she'd never felt before. He'd made her feel like a real woman, alive with desire and passion, not just a naive girl playing at womanhood.

Payton felt a tiny sting of regret that she hadn't accepted his offer of help. She could have used a friend in the outback, someone to show her the ropes, maybe help her find a job. Though her abilities were rather limited, she had spent the last year perfecting her skills as a gourmet cook. She could teach piano and French and Italian. She'd been an excellent rider, winning medals in dressage and show jumping. Surely there was something she could do for an honest wage.

Payton crawled off the bed and walked over to the spot where Brody had stood. She'd make a vow, here and now. From this moment forward, she'd act on her instincts. If she saw something she wanted, she'd go after it. She'd stop planning and start doing. And maybe, once she'd figured out just who she was, away from her parents and Sam, she could get on with the rest of her life.

"You finished with your breakfast?" Angus sauntered into the room, his keys jangling from a ring on his belt. He unlocked the cell door and opened it then stepped inside to collect the tray.

"Thank you," Payton said. "It was good."

He nodded. "Answer a question for me?"

Payton knew she'd have to explain at some point. What was she doing stranded in the middle of the Australian outback without a penny to her name? And what had made her think she could walk out of a restaurant without paying. "Sure. Fire away."

Angus's brow furrowed. "Have you ever been to Graceland?"

"Graceland?" The question didn't take her by surprise considering the police chief's taste in music. "No. But I hear it's supposed to be very nice. I once saw Priscilla Presley in New York, though."

"Priscilla?"

"Yes, I think she was there for Fashion Week. She was hailing a cab on Madison Avenue."

"Well, I'll be buggered! Priscilla Presley. That's almost as good as seeing Elvis." He nodded. "It's always been my dream to visit Graceland. Most folks would go to Disney World or Hollywood or one of those big tall buildings they have in New York City. Me, I'd head straight to Graceland." With a sigh, he stepped out of the cell. "Your debt has been settled, Miss Harwell. You're free to go."

"I am?" She didn't really want to leave. Not before she'd figured out her next move. But then, she had vowed to stop planning and start doing. "Who paid it?"

Angus nodded toward the door. "He's waitin' out front. You'll have to square up with him."

Frowning, Payton grabbed her bag and stuffed her belongings inside, then glanced around the cell to make sure she had everything. Whoever her mysterious benefactor was, she'd find a way to pay him back.

When she reached the porch, she saw a familiar figure waiting for her, dressed in the same faded jeans and wrinkled T-shirt he'd worn earlier. She allowed herself a tiny smile. "Are you the one who—"

Brody grabbed her bag from her hand and slung it over his shoulder. "No need to thank me," he interrupted, motioning toward the dirty Land Rover parked in front of the police station. "We criminals have to stick together, eh?"

Payton walked slowly down the steps, glancing over her shoulder to find him staring at her backside. She reached for the door of the truck, but he rested his hand on hers. "That's the driver's side, sweetheart," he said.

"Sorry," Payton murmured, the heat from his touch

sending a tingle up her arm. He followed her around to the passenger side and helped her in, resting his hand on the small of her back as she climbed up into her seat.

When he slid in behind the wheel, he looked over at her. "Where to?"

"I—I don't know," she said.

"You don't know?"

"I don't have anywhere to go."

"You're giving up your life of crime?" His dark brow arched. "You must have somewhere to go. Everyone is going somewhere."

"Not me," Payton said. "Since I'm out of cash, I can't afford to go anywhere. I need to find a job."

He nodded, then grinned. "All right. Well, I think I know a place that might need some help. As long as you're willing to work hard. What can you do?"

"Anything."

"The local brothel likes to hire talented girls. I could take you over there."

She laughed softly when she saw the smile curling his lips. He had a way of speaking, his accent broad and his voice deep, that made it hard to tell when he was teasing. "Very funny."

"You think I'm kidding? Bilbarra has a legal house of ill repute. And it stays quite busy since women are in short supply in the outback. You could make a decent wage if you were so inclined."

"I'm better with horses than I am with men," Payton said.

"Horses? Well, that sounds promising." He turned the SUV around and headed out of town on the dusty main street. As they drove, the landscape became dry and desolate, an endless vista of…nothing. This was the outback, Payton mused. And she was driving right into the middle of it with a complete stranger. "Where are we going?"

"To my place," he said.

She swallowed hard. So much for acting on instinct. "Your—your place?" Had she just made the biggest mistake of her life? He could drive them out into the middle of nowhere, chain her up and keep her as his sex slave for years and no one would ever know. But then Angus had seen them leave together and if Angus trusted this man with her safety, maybe she could, too. The idea of serving as Brody's sex slave rolled around in her mind for a moment before she shook herself. The thought was intriguing. In truth, any thought that involved Brody's naked body seemed to stick in her head.

"It's my family's place," he explained. "We have a cattle station and we raise horses, too."

"Horses!" she cried. "I'm good with horses. I can groom them and muck out the stalls and feed them…."

"Good," he said. "Then I'm sure we'll have a spot for you." He reached above the visor and pulled out a CD, then popped it into the player in the dash.

Payton watched the countryside pass as they bumped along the dirt roads. Compared to the beautiful scenery on the coast with its lush greenery and ocean views, the outback was a harsh and unforgiving environment. Only occasionally did she see signs of human habitation—a distant house or a windmill on the horizon.

When she wasn't staring out the window, Payton attempted a careful study of the man beside her. He kept his eyes fixed on the road ahead, humming along with the AC/DC songs as he navigated around bumps and potholes.

After an hour of bouncing over rutted roads, the orange juice Payton had gulped down for breakfast had worked its way through her body. "Will it be much farther?" she asked.

"Another half hour," he said.

"Is there a gas station coming up? Maybe a convenience store? Anyplace with a ladies' room?"

Brody pulled the truck to a stop, then pointed out the window. "There's a nice little shrub over there. For privacy." He shrugged. "There isn't a ladies' room between here and the station."

Reluctantly, Payton opened the door. "Don't watch," she said.

"I won't. And if a giant lizard comes wandering by, you just scoot back to the truck flat out."

Payton closed the door. "I can wait."

"The road only gets bumpier," he warned. "I'll keep an eye peeled. If I see anything approaching, I'll hit the horn."

Payton hopped out of the truck and walked gingerly through the scrub to the closest bush. It looked more like tumbleweed than a living plant, but it provided enough cover for her modesty.

She was a long way from home, a long way from marble bathrooms with gold-plated fixtures and expensive French towels. But for the first time in her life, she was in charge of her own destiny. She no longer had to please her parents, or anyone else for that matter. And though she didn't know where she'd be tomorrow or what she'd doing next week, Payton didn't care. Right now, life was one big adventure. And her traveling companion made the adventure a whole lot more interesting.

BRODY LEANED BACK against the front fender of the Land Rover as he stared out at the horizon, taking a long drink from a bottle of water he'd pulled from the Esky in the backseat. He'd been living in the civilized part of Oz for so long that he'd forgotten just how desolate the outback was.

He and his mother had left when he was fourteen. And though he'd returned for his school holidays, he was always anxious to leave again. Now, here he was, back where he started.

He heard footsteps in the gravel at the edge of the road and he turned around as Payton approached, bracing his elbows on the hood of the SUV. "Feel better?"

"Much," she said. She turned slowly, taking in the view. "It's beautiful in a rugged, bleak kind of way. You can breathe out here. The air is so clean."

"Yeah, we have plenty of clean air in Queensland. And we're a big producer of dust. Mozzies and blowies, too." She gave him an odd look. "Mosquitoes and blow flies." He offered her the bottle of water. "And where do you come from?"

She took a long drink of water, then smiled. "The East Coast. Connecticut."

"Is that near New York?"

She nodded. "Yes. Very near. My father works in Manhattan. I went to college at Columbia."

"So you're smart, then?" Smart and beautiful. A deadly combination and one he hadn't really appreciated until now. He'd never considered a brilliant mind an important part of sexual attraction. But as much as he wanted to touch her and kiss her, he also wanted to talk to her. Who was this woman? What was she doing here with him?

"I did my master's thesis on the history of anatomical study in seventeenth-century Dutch artists. I'm not sure how smart that makes me." She glanced around. "Especially out here. Unless you have an art museum filled with the works of Vermeer and Rembrandt."

"We do," he teased. "It's right behind the stables. Doesn't get a lot of visitors, though." Brody drank the last of the water. "So how does a sheila like you end up skint in a place like Bilbarra?"

"Skint?"

"No money."

"Broke," she said. "Flat broke. Probably because I didn't have a lot to start with." She paused. "I'm just a poor grad student trying to see a bit of the world."

"There's not a lot to see in the outback," he said.

"You don't think the scenery out here is spectacular?" Payton asked, pointing to a low range of hills in the distance. "It's wild, untamed. Dangerous. I like that. Don't you?"

He stared down at her face, taking in the simple perfection of her features. "It's gotten a lot nicer since you arrived."

Her eyes met his and Brody held his breath, wondering just how far he could go. He wanted to kiss her. Hell, he'd wanted to kiss her from the moment he'd first seen her. He leaned in, hoping for a sign that she shared the attraction. Her eyes dropped to his mouth and her lips parted slightly. It was all he needed.

Bracing his hands on either side of her body, he pressed her back into the side of the SUV and brought his mouth down on hers. Her lips were soft and cool and fit perfectly with his.

Brody's tongue traced the crease between them before she opened and let him taste her. At first, he thought she might end it all quickly, but then, Payton reached up and ran her fingers through the hair at his nape, sending a shiver through his body and a flood of warmth to his crotch.

The kiss turned intense, fierce and filled with need. God, she was incredible, he thought as his hands skimmed down her arms, then clutched at the hem of her shirt. It had been a while since he'd touched a woman, but he hadn't remembered it being this good. He smoothed his palms beneath her shirt, up her torso to cup her breast. Payton arched toward him, a tiny sigh slipping from her throat.

Brody had seduced his fair share of women, but he'd always tempered his attraction with an underlying suspicion. What did they really want from him? Were they merely interested in bedding a famous footballer? Or did they imagine themselves catching a husband who had the money to provide a fancy lifestyle?

There were no worries with Payton. To her, he was just the guy who'd bailed her out of jail and found her a job. He could let down his guard, at least for a little while. In truth, for the first time in his adult life, he could enjoy a woman without any inhibitions.

When he finally drew back, he found her face flushed and her lips damp. "We should probably go," he said, certain that there would be much more to come. Once he got her to the station, she'd be there for a time. He could afford to seduce her properly.

Her eyes fluttered open and she drew a deep breath. "Yes," she said softly. "Yes, we should."

Brody reached around her and opened the door. But before she could crawl back inside, he stole another kiss, lingering over her lips until he was satisfied that they'd both had enough. He liked kissing her. She had a mouth that was made for that particular pastime.

They drove on for another ten minutes before they spoke again. She cleared her throat and Brody turned to look at her, noting the pretty blush that stained her cheeks. "What?" he asked.

"Nothing," she said.

"You have something you want to say?"

She shook her head. "No."

"Do you regret what just happened?"

She drew another breath and then twisted to face him. "I hope you don't think I just go around kissing strangers, because I don't. It's just that I…" Payton paused. "No, I don't regret it. It was…nice."

"Onya," he replied, satisfied with "nice." Next time it happened, it would be better than nice. Brody grinned. There would be a next time. And a time after that…

"Onya?"

"Good onya," Brody corrected. "Ah…good for you."

"Right, good for me," she said, nodding. "I mean, on me. Good on me."

"No, it doesn't work that way." He grinned.

She smiled and shrugged. "Then, good onya. On you."

"No worries, then?" he said, knowing full well that his kiss was more than welcome.

"No worries," she replied.

Brody chuckled. "And feel free to perv on me whenever you like. Because I wouldn't mind if that happened again. Between us. But I should warn you off on the other blokes."

"Blokes?"

"It's mostly men on the station. There's just our cook and housekeeper, Mary. You'll be the only other woman. The boys on Kerry Creek are root rats of the first order, so keep a watch out for them. They go through women like water." All of a sudden Brody regretted his decision to bring Payton out to the station. He should have flown them both straight back to Fremantle, to his comfortable apartment with the big soft bed and the river views.

Though Callum and Teague weren't quite as bad as the rest of the jackaroos, his brothers wouldn't be immune to Payton's beauty. Women were in short supply in the bush and Brody intended to keep her all to himself. He'd have to find a way to make that clear to his brothers before they got any ideas about seducing her.

"Root rats," she said. "I suppose I could guess at the meaning of that." She sighed. "Are there a lot of root rats where we're going?"

"Yeah," Brody said. "But if any bloke cracks on you, just speak up. I'll sort him out."

"If any guy comes on to me, you'll punch his lights out?"

"That too," Brody said, chuckling. "Don't worry, you'll be safe. I'll watch out for you."

She'd be safe from the other blokes, but could he

guarantee she'd be safe from him? Right now, his thoughts weren't so much focused on protecting her as they were on seducing her. And he couldn't help but wonder what was going through her pretty head.

2

"WILL YOU EXCUSE US for a moment?"

Payton nodded, sitting primly on the edge of her chair as Brody and his brother Callum stepped out of the cluttered office. They didn't go far and their whispered discussion in the hallway soon became loud enough for her to hear.

"And who was whinging about all the work to be done just a few hours ago?" Brody accused. "She claims she knows horses and isn't above mucking out the stables. If she takes care of that, then you've got more help mustering."

"You met her in the jail," Callum shot back. "That might give you a clue to her character."

"She's just down on her luck," Brody said. "She needs a job. I'll vouch for her. If you catch her stealing, I'll haul her back to Bilbarra without a word."

"And what about you?" Callum asked. "If I give her a job, what are you going to do? Just lay about the house all day feeling sorry for yourself?"

"I reckon I'll give you a hand," Brody said. "I've got nothing better to do."

There was a long silence and she heard a curse, though she wasn't sure who it came from. A moment later, the two brothers reappeared in the door. "Brody tells me you're good with horses. You'll be expected to put in a full day."

"I really need this job. I'll work hard, I promise," Payton said. It was the truth, though she didn't want to sound too desperate. This station was the perfect place for her, a good spot to stay until she figured out her next step. She'd have a place to sleep and three decent meals a day. She'd have a job to occupy her time. And then there was Brody. "You won't regret this."

"All right. You can stay in the south bunkhouse," Callum said. "It's got a proper dunny and shower. But you'll have to share it with Gemma."

"Who's Gemma?" Brody asked, frowning.

"The genealogist," Callum explained. "Gemma Moynihan. She's from Ireland, doing some sort of research on the Quinn family. I told her she could stay until she finished her work here."

"No worries," Payton said, adopting the local language. "The bunkhouse will be great."

"All right," Callum said. "You'll start in the stables and you'll lend a hand in the kitchen when Mary needs help. You slack off and you'll earn yourself a ride back to Bilbarra. You work hard and I'll pay you a fair wage."

Payton nodded, relieved that he'd agreed to Brody's plan. It was the first real job she'd ever held and she was determined not to mess up. Her new life began here and now and Payton couldn't help but be a bit excited at the prospect.

Callum glanced at his brother. "Brody will show you around and get you settled. If you have any questions, ask him."

The elder Quinn brother strode out of the office and Brody followed after him. "I'll give her a day. Two at the outside," Payton heard Callum say.

When Brody returned, she pasted a smile on her face. "He's wrong. I'll work hard."

Brody reached out and took her hand, turning it over so he could examine her palm. Running his thumb over the soft skin, he slowly smiled. "You'll need a pair of gloves," he said. "And a proper hat."

Payton laced her fingers through his and gave his hand a squeeze. "Thank you for this. I won't disappoint you."

He hooked his finger beneath her chin, forcing her gaze up to his. At first, she hoped he might kiss her again, but then he must have thought better of it. "No worries. I can't imagine that ever happening."

"No worries," she repeated.

Brody picked up her bag and motioned her toward the door. "Come on. I'll show you what's what. We'll see the homestead first. Maybe Mary will make us a bite."

As they walked through the beautifully furnished room that Brody called the parlor, Payton's attention was caught by a huge oil painting hanging over the fireplace. She walked up to examine it more closely. "This is a beautiful portrait," she said.

"We call him the old man," Brody explained as he stepped up beside her. "His name is Crevan Quinn. He was the first Quinn in Australia. Came on a convict ship when he was nineteen."

"He was a convict?"

Brody nodded. "A bit of a thief, a pickpocket they

say. He had the portrait painted for his seventieth birthday, in the late 1800s. Went all the way to Sydney to sit for it. And then he died the day after it was finished. It's hung in this house ever since. His only son was my great-great-grandfather."

"Backler. I've never heard of the artist," she said. "It's quite lovely."

Brody gave her a dubious look.

"The technique," she said. "The layering of color." She stared at the subject, a man with wild white hair, huge muttonchops and a fierce expression.

"Good thing his looks don't run in the family," Brody said.

"His penchant for crime does," Payton teased.

With that, Brody grabbed her around the waist and gently pushed her back against the mantel. His hand cupped her cheek and he looked down into her eyes. Payton held her breath, caught by the desire in his gaze.

"And where would you be right now if it weren't for my criminal activities?"

"Or mine," she countered. "I'd be without a job and with no prospects for finding one."

"I think that deserves a kiss, don't you?"

"I suppose I could spare one. But don't get greedy."

She pushed up onto her toes and kissed him, not waiting for Brody to make the first move. She liked the taste of him, the way his hands felt on her body. His touch made her feel alive, as if she was doing something far too dangerous for her own good. It was exhilarating and frightening all at once.

Payton looped her fingers in the waistband of his jeans and pulled his hips against hers. He groaned softly as the kiss deepened and their bodies melted into each other. Her hands slipped beneath his T-shirt and she ran her nails up his spine and back down again.

She'd never been so aggressive with a man, but with Brody, all her inhibitions seemed to fall away. There were no rules when she kissed him. Here in Australia, she'd live every day as if it were her last, with no regrets and nothing left undone.

Suddenly, he pushed himself away from her. He sucked in a sharp breath and Payton could see he was trying to regain his self-control. She glanced down and noticed the bulge in the front of his jeans. His reaction pleased her.

"Later," he assured her. He picked up her bag, then grabbed her hand and pulled her along to the front door of the house.

They ran into a man jogging up the front steps and he stopped and pulled off his hat, glancing back and forth between Payton and Brody, before noticing their linked hands. "Hello," he said.

"Teague, this is Payton Harwell. Payton, this is my brother Teague."

He held out his hand and Payton was forced to let go of Brody's to shake it. "Pleasure," he said with a wide grin.

"She's going to be working with the horses," Brody said.

"Good onya," Teague replied. "That's where I'll be working for the next few days. You have much experience with stock ponies?"

Payton shook her head, grateful for the welcome but worried that she might not prove herself useful. "No.

But I've been around horses since I was six or seven. Show jumpers. But horses are horses. They all have four legs and a tail, right?"

Teague chuckled, as if pleased with her little joke. "Yeah. They usually do. So I guess I can't give you any of our three-legged ponies."

Payton's eyes went wide.

"Crocs," Teague said, a serious expression on his face. "They'll eat the legs right off a pony if you let them. One leg we can deal with. But a two-legged stock pony just doesn't work."

"Oh, no," Payton said. "That's horrible. Can't you—"

"Don't be a dipstick, Teague." Brody shook his head.

An older woman appeared at the screen door. "Doc Daley is on the phone," she said to Teague, motioning him inside. "Says it's an emergency and he's tied up in surgery this afternoon."

Teague frowned, shaking his head. "Probably another croc attack," he said. "Another three-legged pony. Mary, have you met Brody's new friend?"

The woman stepped out onto the porch, a smile twitching at the corners of her mouth. She wiped her hands on her apron, then smoothed a strand of gray hair from her temple. "Well, now. It is a pleasure to meet you, dear. I'm Mary Hastings. No matter what these Quinn boys tell you, I'm the one in charge here."

Payton shook her outstretched hand. "Payton Harwell."

"Ah, an American. We seem to be attracting an interesting group of ladies. First, an Irish lass and now a Yank. If you need anything, you come to me, dear. We girls have to stick together." She leaned forward and lowered her voice. "And don't believe a word about those three-legged ponies. These boys get too cheeky."

Teague grabbed Mary around the waist and planted a kiss on her cheek. "And don't you love it? Don't worry, Mary, you're still my girl."

Brody took Payton's hand and led her off the porch. "Come on, I'll show you the bunkhouse."

"It was a pleasure meeting you," Payton said, waving at Teague and Mary.

"See ya later, Payton," Teague called.

"When you're settled, you come back to the kitchen for tea," Mary called.

They walked together to the south bunkhouse, a low building set near a small grove of trees and a neatly tilled vegetable garden. "That's Mary's garden," he said. "You might want to avoid walking by when she's working. She'll have you pulling weeds all day long."

"She's nice," Payton said.

"After my mum left the station, my dad hired her. She's kept the house running."

"Are your parents divorced?"

He shook his head. "Nope. They're living together in Sydney. But there was a time when they were separated, my dad here and Mum in the city. Station life is hard, especially for women."

Payton gave him a sideways glance, wondering if he was warning her off. She was just looking for a job. She didn't intend to spend the rest of her life in the Australian outback. "I can imagine," she replied.

Brody opened the front door of the bunkhouse, then stepped back to let her enter. Payton found the interior simple but clean. In one corner of the room, several

overstuffed chairs were gathered around a small iron
stove. There was a scarred desk beneath one of the
windows and a dry sink beneath another, complete with
bowl and pitcher. An old wardrobe stood near the
backdoor. Each of the three walls held a bunk bed,
crudely constructed of rough planks and a pair of mat-
tresses. One of the lower bunks was made up with a
colorful quilt and two pillows.

"That must be where the genealogy lady is sleeping,"
Brody said. "Bedding is in the chest at the end of the
bunk. The dunny is out back, through that door."

"The dunny."

"The toilet. There's a shower back there, too." He
walked over to the wardrobe and rummaged through the
contents until he found a pair of gloves and an old felt
hat, like the one his brother Teague wore.

Brody set the hat on her head and handed her the
gloves. "There you go," he said, tugging on the brim.
"Pretty spiffy."

"I'd like to get to work," she said.

"You don't have to. It's your first day. Take some
time and settle in. We'll have some lunch."

"No, I'm ready to start," she insisted, well aware
that she'd have to prove herself to Callum.

"You're not really dressed properly. We'll need to
find you something to wear."

"I don't really have anything else along," Payton
said, glancing down at the peasant blouse and jeans
she'd bought in Brisbane. "Just a few dresses. This will
have to do for now. I'll find something later."

"All right," he said with a shrug. "Let's go."

They walked out of the bunkhouse and through the

dusty yard. The station was almost like a small village. Brody pointed out each paddock and barn and shed, telling her what function it served. There were two more bunkhouses for the stockmen and a small cottage for the head stockman.

The stables consisted of a long building with stalls along one side and tack, feed and supplies stored on the opposite side. "We breed stock ponies here, so we keep a lot of mares. We break the ponies and then sell them to stations all around Queensland. Kerry Creek ponies fetch a good price."

Payton pulled on her gloves and braced her hands on her hips. "All right. Well, I'd better jump right in." She spotted a pitchfork in a corner and grabbed it. "I guess I'll see you later."

He seemed to be a bit surprised that she was blowing him off so quickly. Though Payton found him wildly attractive, she needed to keep this job and first impressions would count. If she had to ignore her desires for a few hours, it was a small price to pay.

"We eat dinner at six this time of year. I'll come and fetch you."

"That's all right," Payton said. "I'll find my way."

He turned and walked out of the stable. Payton folded her hands over the end of the pitchfork and watched his retreat. Her girlfriends had always told her how hot Sam was and she'd never quite understood what they meant. Sam was handsome, but Brody Quinn was hot. He oozed masculinity from every pore.

She tried to imagine him without the T-shirt, without the jeans, without any clothes at all. A shiver skittered down her spine and she felt her pulse quicken. Sleeping with the boss was never a good thing. But was Brody her boss or was Callum?

Payton made a mental note to find out as soon as she could. For now, she had a bed and free meals and something to occupy her time—along with a man who made her heart race and her body tingle. What more did she need?

LIKE EVERYONE ELSE at Kerry Creek, Brody had worked the station from the time he'd been able to walk. He'd started in the garden with his mother, then moved to the stables and on to working with the stock as soon as he could ride. But he'd spent most of his teen years in the city, and once he'd signed his first pro contract, he'd made only occasional visits to Queensland, stopping in before a holiday spent surfing or diving on the Great Barrier Reef.

His brothers teased him, insisting that city life had made him soft. Maybe it had. But now that he was living on the station again, it was all coming back to him. He'd spent the afternoon repairing fences with the newest jackaroo, a kid named Davey Thompson, who'd wandered in a few months before to join his older brother, Skip, on the station.

Davey had kept up a constant stream of chatter, moving from women to music to cars and back again. One thing was quite clear. He was glad to have moved up in the pecking order, his stable job handed off to Payton, who was now the lowest in seniority.

"That new girl, she's a pretty sheila," he said as he picked up a roll of barbed wire. "She has nice hair. All long and curly."

"You just steer clear of her," Brody warned.

"What? She's your girl?"

"As far as you're concerned, yes," Brody said. "She's my girl."

"No worries," Davey replied with a grin. "But does she have a sister? If she does, I wouldn't mind an introduction."

They worked until sunset, hauling their gear with quad bikes rather than on horseback. Since his father had left the station to join his mother in Sydney four years ago, Callum had taken steps to modernize the operation and his ideas had made the work at least a bit more enjoyable.

Brody and Davey unloaded the gear from the ATVs, then headed to the big house for dinner. Mary fed everyone at the large table in the kitchen, preparing the heartiest meal at the end of the workday. Brody took time to wash up at the outdoor sink before going inside.

He'd expected to see Payton there, waiting for him, but she wasn't seated at the table. The other new arrival was the genealogist from Ireland. He'd expected some gray-haired lady with sensible shoes and little reading glasses perched on her nose. Instead, he found himself smiling at a woman almost as beautiful as Payton.

"Gemma Moynihan," she said in a lilting Irish accent. "And you must be Brody. I can see the family resemblance."

"Gemma," Brody repeated. He glanced over at his brother Callum, only to find him staring at them both, a tense expression on his face. It was easy to see why Cal had been on edge. His oldest brother had always been obsessed with the station. But the choice to work or to spend time with Gemma the genealogist was probably causing him to seriously question his work ethic.

"Have you met Payton?" Brody asked, suppressing a grin.

"Yes, I have," Gemma said.

"Is she coming in to eat?"

"I don't know. She was lying in her bunk when I left. She looked knackered."

"Maybe I should take her something," Brody suggested, stepping away from the table.

This brought amused glances from the rest of the stockmen, but Brody didn't care. He grabbed a plate and loaded it with beef and potatoes, covering the entire meal with a portion of gravy. Grabbing utensils and a couple of beers, he headed out to the ladies' bunkhouse.

He found Payton curled up on her bunk sound asleep. He set the meal on the floor beside the bed, then pulled up a chair, straddling it. Reaching out, Brody brushed a strand of hair from her eyes. Her lashes fluttered and she gazed up at him.

"Morning," he said.

Payton pushed up on her elbow looking worried. "Is it morning already?"

He laughed. "No. I brought you some dinner. Are you all right?"

She sat up, wincing as she moved. "Yes. I'm fine. I'm just not used to shoveling horse poop for four hours." She groaned, rubbing her shoulder. "I was just going to lie down for a minute, and I must have fallen asleep."

"Come here," Brody said, swinging the chair around and patting the seat.

When she was seated, he handed her the plate, then stepped behind her and began to massage her sore shoulders. "Oh, that's nice," she said, tipping her head back and closing her eyes. Her silky curls fell across his hands. "Right there."

He rubbed a little harder at her nape, brushing her hair over her shoulder. "Here?"

"Mmm," she said.

"Eat your dinner before it gets cold."

She glanced down at the plate, then scooped up a forkful of beef and potatoes. "This is good," she said as she chewed. "I didn't realize how hungry I was. Don't you want some?"

"You eat," he said. "I'll go back and get another plate."

She reached down and grabbed a bottle of beer, then attempted to twist off the cap. When she couldn't, she handed it to him. "What did you do today?"

"Repaired fences," Brody said.

"What time does work start in the morning?"

"The stockmen are usually up at dawn. But you could probably sleep later, if you like. The stables aren't going anywhere."

"No, I'll get up with everyone else."

"I don't reckon Cal expects you to put in stockman's hours."

"What else is there to do except work and eat and sleep?" Payton asked.

Brody bent over her shoulder and sent her a devilish grin. "I can think of a few things," he whispered.

She filled a fork with food, then held it up to him, and he took a bite of her dinner. "Other than that, what do you do with your free time?"

"We're five hours from the nearest movie theater in Brisbane, but we've got DVDs to watch. Cal favors westerns, I like gangster movies and Teague prefers science fiction." He paused. "We've got a pool," he added. "Sometimes we go swimming when the weather is warm."

"I didn't see a pool."

"It's not a swimming pool, more like a watering hole. And Cal put in a hot tub out back. That's nice now that the nights are a bit cooler."

"Oh, that sounds like heaven," she said.

"Finish your supper and we'll go for a dip."

"I don't have a swimsuit."

"You won't need one," Brody said.

"I'm sure that will create a good impression," she replied.

To his surprise, she finished the entire plate in ten short minutes, then drank her beer and his. Through it all, she asked questions about the station and he did his best to answer. She'd just assumed he'd worked the station his whole life, and he wasn't going to tell her differently, at least not yet.

He had his secrets, but Payton Harwell had her own. When he asked for details about her life in the States, she always gave him some airy-fairy answer. After fifteen minutes of questioning, he realized he didn't know much more than he'd learned on their ride to the station. But the more beer she drank, the more forthcoming she became.

"Let's go," he said, anxious to spend some time in a location more conducive to seduction. "The hot water will make you feel better."

"Later," she said. "I just want to lie down for a bit."

She crawled back into her bunk and patted the spot beside her. "Just for a minute. Then we'll go."

Brody crawled into the tiny bunk, and he had to wrap his arms around her just to keep from falling on the floor. He smoothed his hands over her hair and she looked up at him and smiled. "Who are you, Payton Harwell?" he murmured.

"I don't know," she said with a soft sigh. "If you figure it out, be sure to fill me in."

He bent closer and kissed her, this time allowing himself to relax and enjoy the experience. His hands roamed over her body, slipping beneath the waistband of her jeans to cup her backside. Brody pulled her beneath him, his shaft growing harder as the kiss deepened.

His hips pressed into hers and he slowly began to move, creating a delicious friction. He remembered the first time he'd done this with a girl and the rather surprising results. But thankfully, he'd managed to acquire a bit more self-control over the years. Still, the feel of her beneath him, her leg pulled up alongside his, teased at that control. Brody knew Gemma might be back at any second, but he didn't care.

Payton slipped her hand beneath the hem of his shirt. She smoothed her palms up his chest, then trailed her fingertips down his belly. He groaned softly when she slid her hand lower, across the front of his jeans, then back again. Somehow, it all seemed more intense, more pleasurable, with clothing between them and the chance of discovery.

He pulled her shirt over her shoulder, exposing a delicious curve of flesh. Pressing his mouth to the base of her neck, he slowly worked his way down, to the tops of her breasts, left exposed by her lacy bra.

He slid lower along her body, his lips teasing at her nipple through the lace and satin. Payton furrowed her fingers through his hair and he sucked gently, until she moaned in response.

He fought the urge to strip off all their clothes, knowing they didn't have much privacy in a shared bunkhouse. Perhaps Gemma would be occupied with Callum for the rest of the evening. Maybe she'd choose to spend the night in his bed instead of her own. But their privacy was cut short when he heard the front door open.

"Sorry," Gemma called. "I'll come back later."

When the door closed behind Gemma, he drew back and looked into Payton's eyes. She forced a smile. "Maybe you should go," she said.

"Maybe you should come with me," he suggested. He curled up against her, nuzzling his face into the curve of her neck. "I have a very large bed in my room. And a strong lock on the door. We won't be disturbed."

"We won't get any sleep, either," Payton said.

"That's the point, isn't it?"

She sighed softly and he waited for her decision. But after a minute or two, Brody realized that she'd fallen asleep. Her breathing had grown soft and even and the arm resting on his hip had gone limp.

He bit back a curse, then pressed a kiss to her forehead. She stirred for a moment, her eyes fluttering. "I'm going to go. You need your sleep. I'll see you in the morning."

"Morning," she sighed.

Reluctantly, he untangled himself from her embrace, rolled off the bed and tugged his shirt down. He turned to look at Payton, her dark hair fanned out over the pillow, her hand curled over her face.

If he wasn't such a gentleman, he'd pick her up, carry her to his bedroom and make love to her all night long. But he had time. And when it happened, they'd both be awake and completely aware of what they were doing. It would be good between them. Maybe better than it had ever been with any other woman.

For that, Brody was willing to wait.

PAYTON GRABBED the hoof pick, then pushed the horse up against the side of the stall with her shoulder. Lifting the gelding's front leg, she held its hoof between her thighs and began to clean out the debris between the frog and the bars.

Unlike the horses she rode for show, the horses on the station didn't spend much time in the stable. They were brought in after a day's work and then quickly groomed and sent out to a large paddock where they were fed. The ground was dry and the stable kept clean, so there was no need for a farrier and horseshoes.

The Kerry Creek horses were a sturdy lot, most gentle and accommodating—the furthest thing from the pampered, high-spirited show horses she'd learned to ride. Brody had informed her that the stockmen were responsible for the daily care of their own mounts, but she was expected to care for the remainder in the paddock and the stables—nearly forty by her count.

These included mares that were in foal and the colts who were yet to be broken, along with at least ten extra stock ponies. She'd also spend part of each day in the tack room, keeping the stockmen's saddles and bridles in good working order. And with what time was left over, she'd turn her attention to mixing feed and keeping the stables tidy.

The dry season was the busiest of all on a cattle station. The stockmen were getting ready to bring the cattle in for the yearly mustering, setting off to the far corners of the station to gather the herd, sometimes staying out three or four days. The new calves would be examined, vaccinated, tagged and branded with the *K* that signified Kerry Creek station.

The horses that were part of the breeding operation were pastured closer to the homestead where they could be watched closely and brought inside as their time grew near. Foals that were dropped outside could be easy prey for dingoes.

"You look like you know what you're doing."

Payton glanced up to see Brody's brother Teague standing just outside the stall, his shoulder braced against a post, his arms crossed over his chest. Like Brody and Callum, he was gorgeous. But unlike Brody, he didn't send shivers of desire coursing through her body, nor did she spend hours thinking about kissing him.

She shoved the sleeves of her oversize work shirt above her elbows, then nodded. "It's a whole different kind of horse," she said with a smile. "They have a wonderful temperament."

"That's the way we breed them and train them," he said. "And for stamina and strength and agility. They need to be able to last all day long. Sometimes all week."

Payton continued her work. "What are the bloodlines?"

"Originally thoroughbreds and Arabians with some Welsh mountain and Timor pony thrown in."

"When do they foal?"

"They tend to start in September and go through the first of the year. Usually right after mustering ends, we start in with foaling."

"Davey said the colt in the next stall has been sold. He's beautiful."

"He's going to be trained as a show horse. Some of our horses are used for polocrosse. And some for campdrafting."

Payton set the horse's hoof onto the concrete floor and straightened, brushing her hair out of her eyes. "What's that?"

"Besides Aussie-rules football, polocrosse and campdrafting are the only native Aussie sports. Polocrosse is a mix of polo, lacrosse and netball. And I reckon campdrafting is kind of like your rodeo riding. The horse and rider cut a calf from the herd, then they have to maneuver it around a series of posts."

"I'd like to see that," she said.

"I'll take you sometime," Teague promised. "There's a campdrafting event in Muttaburra in August if you're still around."

"I'd like to try it."

"Then I'll teach you."

"Teach her what?"

Brody appeared at his brother's side. He was dressed in traditional stockman's attire, a work shirt, canvas jacket, jeans. He wore a felt hat on his head and his hands were clad in well-worn leather gloves. She hadn't seen him since the previous evening and she'd forgotten just how beautiful he was.

"Hey, little brother. Where have you been?"

"I went out with Davey to fix the windmill in the high pasture."

Teague clapped his brother on the back. "Good to see you putting in an honest day's work." He touched the brim of his hat and nodded at Payton. "I've got a call. I'll see you later, Payton. Maybe you can give me a hand tomorrow morning. I've got vaccinations to do on the yearlings."

"Sure," Payton said. "I'd be happy to help."

He nodded again. "I think I'll like having you here." Teague turned to Brody, arching an eyebrow and examining him critically. "Have you had all your shots?"

Payton watched Brody's jaw grow tense. As the youngest brother, he probably had to put up with a greater share of the teasing. "Don't mind Teague," Brody said as his brother turned and walked away. "He has a bad habit of yabbering to anyone who'll listen."

"So, is Teague in charge of the horse-breeding operation?"

"When he's around. He's a vet."

"A veterinarian? Really?"

Brody nodded. "He's usually flying from station to station. He spends a few days at home, then takes off again. He's the brilliant one in the family."

"He's nice," Payton murmured. She met Brody's gaze and her breath stopped in her throat. It was all there, the desire, the need and even a tiny hint of jealousy. She drew a ragged breath as he crossed the short distance between them to pull her into his arms.

Payton had tried to put all of this out of her head. From the moment she woke up that morning she'd been waiting to touch him, to taste him. It had been eight hours of sheer torture and now she felt the tension in her body release as their mouths met.

The more she saw of him, the more difficult it was to resist him. And yet, that didn't frighten or confuse her. She didn't need to figure out the consequences of her every action and reaction. She could kiss Brody and that was all it was, a kiss. It felt good to cast aside her penchant for planning and just go with the flow.

But how long could that last? How long before a simple fling turned into something more complicated? Her feelings for him were already so intense, her desire undeniable. She'd promised herself that she'd be guided by her instincts, and every instinct told her to enjoy their time together. They didn't need to make promises to each other. This was enough.

He cupped her face in his palms and drew her deeply into the kiss, as if desperate to possess her. Payton was stunned at how easy it was to stoke his need. There was no hesitation, nothing she held back. Though she barely knew Brody, she felt a connection with him that she'd never shared with a man before.

He pulled her out of the stall, his hands tight around her waist. Stumbling back, they fell into a pile of straw, their mouths still frantically searching for the perfect manifestation of their need. He tossed his hat aside, then tugged off his gloves, his hands immediately moving to cup her backside. Though Payton knew their privacy in the stable wasn't certain, she didn't care. All that mattered was his touch, his fingers tearing at her shirt until he exposed the curve of her shoulder.

His teeth grazed her skin and Payton tipped her head back, inviting him to take more. There were moments when she acted on instinct, as if this woman had always been buried deep inside her and was just waiting to get out. And then, at other times, she felt like a teenager, fumbling her way though her first sexual experience.

He excited her and frightened her all at once. And yet, she pushed aside her fears, rushing headlong into her desire, aching to experience release. Payton tugged at his jacket, pulling it over his arms until she could unbutton his shirt.

"Too many clothes," she murmured as she brushed aside the shirt and placed a kiss in the center of his chest. He was so magnificent, she mused, his skin deeply tanned and his body finely muscled. Her lips found one of his nipples and she circled it with her tongue.

Brody ran his fingers through her hair, sighing her name softly as if urging her on. Slowly, Payton worked her way lower, trailing kisses over his abdomen. But before she could go farther, she heard the clip-clop of hooves on the concrete floor of the stable.

She looked up to find Callum standing just inside the stable door, his horse's reins dangling from his fingers. With a soft cry, Payton scrambled to her feet, brushing the straw from her clothes and trying to adjust her shirt. Callum arched a brow as he looked down at Brody. "I can come back later," he said slowly.

Brody shook his head, cursing. "No. Feel free. We were just…talking."

"Oh, is that what they call it?" Callum asked. He pulled his horse along until he stopped in front of Payton. "Is my brother bothering you? If he is, you can just tell him to leave."

Callum was always so serious that Payton couldn't tell if he was angry or just teasing. She gave him an apologetic smile. "It—it won't happen again," she said. "I'm sorry."

Callum reached up and plucked a piece of straw from her hair and handed it to her, a grin quirking at the corners of his mouth. Payton felt her cheeks warm and she took the reins from his hand. "I'll take care of your horse," she mumbled.

Tugging at the bit, she pulled the horse along the length of the stable, hoping to get as far away from the two brothers as possible. She would not keep this job for long if she continued to show such a blatant disrespect for her employer.

And she needed this job! She wasn't ready to go home. The thought of facing her family and Sam was just too much for her right now. Here, on the station, she felt useful, which made her far happier than she'd been in a very long time.

But was it the work that made her happy or was it her growing infatuation with Brody Quinn? She'd be deluding herself if she ignored his part in this. Glancing back, she caught sight of Callum and Brody, deep in conversation, Callum gesturing with his gloved hands and Brody watching him with an indolent expression.

She barely knew the Quinn brothers, but the family dynamics were quite evident. Callum was the caretaker, the responsible brother whose only focus was the success of the station. Teague was the charmer, the smart, funny one with the ready smile and witty conversation.

And Brody…well, he was a little more difficult to define. He seemed to be the rebel of the family, a bit of an outsider. Payton couldn't understand why he stayed on the station when it was so obvious that it wasn't his favorite place to be.

She tied Callum's horse up to a nearby post and began to remove the saddle. When she straightened from unbuckling the cinch, she found Brody standing behind her. He gently turned her around to face him, then bent lower and kissed her.

"Sorry about that," he said, reaching out to smooth his hand over her hair.

"We can't do that again," she said, looking up at him. "I need this job, Brody."

"You're not going to lose your job," he said. "Cal doesn't care. He's so preoccupied with Gemma, he doesn't have time to worry about us."

"*I* care." Turning back to Callum's mount, she pulled the saddle off and set it on a bale of straw. "I like working here. And I need to pay you back for taking care of my debts."

"Cal can't complain about what you do when you're finished working, can he?"

"No," she said, setting the saddle pad on top of the saddle. "I guess not."

"All right, then. We'll just have to confine ourselves to the hours before breakfast and after dinner. And we're going to have to find a place that offers some privacy." He grabbed the saddle and hoisted it over his shoulder. "Why don't you let me take care of Cal's horse and you can finish what you were doing earlier. Then we'll go eat."

"You don't have to help me."

"Yes I do," Brody said. "Because the sooner you finish, the sooner I'll have you all to myself."

Perhaps he was right. As long as she finished her work, Callum couldn't begrudge her evenings spent with Brody. "Okay."

Her second day of work had been as exhausting as her first. But the prospect of spending time alone with Brody gave her a sudden surge of energy. She'd fallen asleep in his arms last night then woken up to an empty bed. She wasn't about to do that two nights in a row. "It's a date."

"Good." He grabbed the blanket and headed toward the tack room.

Payton watched him, smiling to herself. There was something so attractive about a man who actually worked for a living, a man who used his body the way it was meant to be used—for hard labor…and seduction. Brody was dirty and sweaty, yet she wanted him more than she'd ever wanted a man in her life.

3

BRODY DROPPED the phone into the cradle, then pushed back in Callum's desk chair, linking his hands behind his head. He hadn't bothered to pick up his messages on his mobile phone since reception in Bilbarra and at the station was nonexistent. But remotely checking the voice mail of his home phone at his apartment in Fremantle had brought an interesting development.

Cursing softly, he closed his eyes, a tightly held breath escaping his chest. When he'd left Fremantle, the team doctors had assured him there was no chance he would ever play football again. But now, a doctor in Los Angeles had developed a surgery that offered a way to reconstruct his bum knee.

Why now, why after he'd resigned himself to his fate? Why even tempt him with the possibility of regaining everything he'd lost? Brody knew it would be a long shot at best. And even if the surgery was successful, there'd be months, maybe a year or two, of rehab. Was he really willing to put in the time, just for another chance to play?

He didn't really have a choice. Brody had never been cut out for station life. The problem was he didn't have any options beyond football and stockman's work. He could invest in a business before he retired, but he wasn't sure what he wanted to buy. Or he could go to university and learn something new, but he was too old to go back to being a student.

"You never were one to plan ahead," he muttered to himself.

"Hey, dinner is on the table," Callum said, poking his head in the door. "Best be quick or Davey'll snag the seat next to your girl."

"She isn't my girl," Brody said, running his hand through his hair.

Callum shrugged. "I'm sure the boys will be happy to hear that. They've been carrying on like pork chops since she and Gemma arrived."

"All right, she *is* my girl. For now. And I expect that pretty Irish thing won't be spending much time with the boys, either. I see the way you stare at her. Explain to me again what she's doing here?"

"Research," Callum said. "She's working for some distant relative of ours on a family history. I guess one branch of the family left Ireland for the States and another branch came here. She's been going over all the old records for the station."

"What does that have to do with family history?" Brody asked.

"I don't know." He drew a deep breath. "I don't really care. As long as it keeps her here."

"Maybe she really fancies Teague. He's always been the looker in the family."

"Teague's got something else going," Callum murmured. "I was up early this morning and I saw him come in just before sunrise. There's not an available woman, besides Gemma, Payton and Mary, within fifty kilometers of this station, but he sure looked well satisfied."

"Maybe he's clearing the cobwebs at the brothel, or with a married lady," Brody said.

Callum shook his head. "Teague wouldn't do that. He's too bloody honorable. And why would he when he can usually have any woman he wants?" Callum paused. "I'm just worried he—"

"What?" Brody asked.

"I heard Hayley Fraser's back on her grandfather's station. Teague's always been a bit jelly kneed when it comes to her. First love and all that."

"Marrying Teague off to Hayley would solve all your problems." Brody teased. "The Frasers would be family, and family don't sue family." He pushed away from the desk. "If that's who he's messing with, he should be encouraged, don't you think?"

Callum cursed softly. "And maybe Fraser is using his granddaughter to mess with us," he shot back. "Did you ever consider that? Maybe he thinks if he can't get the land in court, he'll get it another way."

"How?"

"I don't know. Blackmail. Extortion. Fraser will go after that land any way he can. I just hope Teague doesn't get caught in the crossfire."

"Come on, Cal, you're talking crazy now. This feud has gone on for so long that nobody can see straight."

"I'm not going to surrender to Harry Fraser," Cal said. "That land belongs to the Quinns and we're not going to lose it while I'm in charge." He nodded his head. "Come on, dinner is ready. Mary won't wait."

Brody stared after him, then slowly stood. There were times when Brody wondered how Cal handled all the pressures of running the station. So many people depended on him. His parents took a share of the station income. Then there were the stockmen who expected to be paid. Teague's practice wouldn't make decent money for a few years, so he traded vet services for room and board. And now Brody was sponging off Callum. From now on, he'd make a better effort to pull his own weight.

The kitchen was already noisy when Brody walked in, filled with the usual dinner guests—the stockmen, Teague and Mary, and now Gemma and Payton.

With women at the table, the conversation had become much more civilized. Brody dislodged one of the jackaroos from the chair next to Payton, then sat down beside her. Unlike the majority of the men, Brody unfolded his serviette and placed it on his lap instead of stuffing it down the front of his shirt.

"What exactly is a B and S?" Gemma asked.

"Bachelors and Spinsters Ball," Teague explained as he grabbed a piece of bread and slathered it with butter. "All the unmarried people get together for a weekend of silliness. If you're not an Aussie, I don't think I'd recommend it. Foreigners might not have the fortitude to survive the weekend."

"But it sounds like fun," Payton said, leaning forward and bracing her elbows on the table. "I always loved balls and dances and cotill—" She stopped short, as if she'd suddenly revealed too much. Forcing a smile, she continued, "Is it formal or semiformal?"

"Tell her, Teague," Brody insisted, chuckling to

himself. Though Payton hadn't said much, she had revealed something of value this time out. She'd either enjoyed a high-class upbringing or she was a professional princess. He'd never known a single person who'd been to a real ball.

"It's not really a ball, the way you're thinking," Teague explained. "And by silliness, I mean debauchery."

"It's more like a big outdoor party," Callum explained.

Teague nodded. "There's music and drinking and… well, the whole idea is to get pissed, have a good time and hopefully enjoy a shag at the end of the night."

Gemma and Payton looked at each other, shocked expressions on their faces. "Have sex?" Payton asked.

Teague nodded. "Yeah, I guess that's the point. Lots of blokes bring their swag along for just that purpose. Life gets real lonely in the outback."

"What is swag?" Gemma asked. "Money? Do you pay for sex?"

"It's a sleeping roll," Brody explained. "Camping gear. Believe me, you don't want to go to the B and S. It gets feral."

"Filthy is a better word for it," Mary said as she set a bowl of peas next to Brody. She took her spot at the far end of the table. "If you don't want to get dirty or pawed, I wouldn't recommend it. And the loos are disgusting."

"I heard they're going to do something about that," Callum commented. "The organizers reckon they'll get a better class of sheilas if they guarantee clean toilets. They're going to hire someone to keep them tidy."

"I remember last year, Jack made his own loo with

a milk crate and a dunny seat," Teague said. "All the girls were wild for it. He'd let 'em use it, then try to charm them out of their grundies. Such a player, our Jack."

The lanky stockman shook his head, his long hair falling into his eyes. "I won't be able to compete with trailer toilets," Jack said glumly.

"It might be fun," Payton said. She turned to Gemma. "What do you think? When in Australia, do as the Aussies do?"

Gemma laughed. "We'd have to get something nice to wear."

"I have dresses," Payton said. "I need work clothes. I can't wear Davey's castoffs forever. Not that I don't appreciate the loan," she said, giving the kid a warm smile.

"I have to fly to Brisbane in a few days. I could take you shopping," Teague offered.

"Hang on there," Callum interrupted. "Gemma and Payton are not going to Bachelors and Spinsters."

"We won't participate," Gemma said. "We'll just go to…observe. Think of it as sightseeing. Or anthropological research."

"If you want to see the real sights of Australia, I'll take you," Teague said. "Queensland is beautiful from the air."

"There's an idea," Callum said. "You'd be much safer in a plane piloted by our brother than at Bachelors and Spinsters."

Brody slipped his hand beneath the table and smoothed his palm along Payton's thigh. "We could always send Mary to the ball. It's about time she got off this station and had a bit of fun. There are plenty of blokes who'd fancy a dance with our Mary."

The older woman's cheeks turned bright red and she hushed the laughter around the table. "Maybe I will," she said, giving them all a haughty expression. "I'd venture to say I could outdance all you boys."

The rest of the dinner conversation focused on the sights that every visitor in Australia needed to see, the Bachelors and Spinsters forgotten. Everyone at the table had an opinion about the finest tourist sights, both in and outside of Queensland. By the time they'd finished dessert, Teague had a long list, starting with a trip to Brisbane.

As Mary began to clear the table, Brody pushed back, then slid Payton's chair out for her. The rest of the hands looked at him in disbelief. "What are you all gawking at? Some of us here have good manners," Brody said.

The men quickly scrambled to their feet and rushed to Gemma's chair, but Callum waved them off. In truth, Brody's actions had nothing to do with manners. He wanted Payton all to himself and the faster that happened the better. But she seemed determined to keep him waiting.

"I'm going to help Mary clean up," she said, taking his plate and hers.

"Go along with you now. I have all the help I can handle," Mary said. "Davey promised to lend a hand."

Brody squeezed her elbow and pulled her along, out the backdoor to the porch that ran the width of the house. He found a dark corner and pushed her back against the house, then kissed her long and hard, his hands trapping her arms on either side of her head, his hips pressing into hers.

"I've been wanting to do that since I sat down next to you." He groaned.

Payton clutched the front of his shirt, then pushed up onto her toes and kissed him back. "Me, too," she said breathlessly. "I know where we can go. Someplace private."

This time, she pulled *him* along. They headed toward the stables, now dark and silent. When they got inside, Payton fumbled around in the gloom. "There's a flashlight here somewhere."

Brody grabbed it from a shelf above her head and flipped it on, holding it under his chin. "It's called a torch," he said.

Payton held out her hand and he gave it to her. They made their way down the length of the stable to an empty stall. She slid the door open and stepped inside. To Brody's surprise, she'd laid blankets over a mound of straw and arranged a few bales for seating.

"You did this?"

Payton nodded. "When you left to take the phone call. I figured we wouldn't have any privacy in the bunkhouse with Gemma there."

"And what do you plan to do with me once you've lured me inside?" he teased.

"I think we should get to know each other a little better," she said. She caught the front of his shirt and pulled him toward her. "There's so much I don't know about you. So many questions I have to ask."

"You want to talk?"

She nodded.

"I don't know anything about you," he said, smiling down at her. "Tell me something. Anything"

"My birthday is August tenth," she said. "I'm going to be twenty-six."

"Something more interesting," he demanded, his breath warm against her mouth.

"I broke my arm when I fell off my horse. I was seventeen. I had to have surgery." She pointed to her elbow. "I have a scar."

He ran his fingers through her hair and she closed her eyes and tipped her head back. "Something more intimate," he urged, pressing his lips to her throat.

"I lost my virginity in a stable. The Grand Prix in 2001. A month before I broke my arm. I was seduced by a Brazilian stable hand with the most beautiful blue eyes."

"Funny," Brody replied. "I lost mine in the back of my mother's car after footy practice. I was fifteen and she was older. Eighteen, if I recall."

Payton worked at the buttons of his shirt and when they were all undone, she looked up at him. "What else?"

Brody chuckled. "I think we can leave the questions until later."

"So you know what you're doing?" she whispered.

Somehow, he found her question incredibly intriguing. "Yes," he replied as she slid his shirt over his shoulders. "I know exactly what I'm doing. Do you?"

She nodded. "Close the door."

Brody moved to do as she asked, then froze. Hell, he didn't know what he was doing. He hadn't even bothered to bring along protection. "Sorry," he said, turning to face her. "Wait here. I'll be right back."

He tugged his shirt back on, then took the torch from her hand. He jogged back to the house and when he got to the kitchen, he found Mary sitting alone at the table, reading a magazine and sipping a cup of coffee.

"Back so soon?" she asked.

"It's a little chilly out. I need to get a jacket for Payton. Wouldn't want her to catch a cold."

"You're a gentleman," she said, glancing up. "And I hope you'll use a condom. Safe sex and all."

Brody stopped short. Mary had slipped into the role of mother to Callum and Teague after their own mother had moved off the station. And now that Brody had returned, she'd welcomed him as a surrogate son and was equally as protective. "Yes, I won't forget that. Not that it's any of your business."

After retrieving the condoms and a jacket from his room, Brody jogged back out to the stables. He found Payton standing at the stable door waiting.

"What was so impor—" She stopped when he held up the string of three condoms. "Oh. Well, that's probably a good idea."

He drew her into his arms and they stumbled toward the stall. After they stepped inside, Payton pulled the door closed. The light from the torch, when reflected off the walls of the stable, was just enough to see by. Suddenly, he felt nervous, just as he had the first time he'd been with a girl.

This was silly. There had been plenty of women in his life since then. But none of them had ever affected him the way Payton did. Was it because she was still a stranger? That couldn't be it. Or was it because she seemed more exotic, different from the women he usually took to his bed?

She was well educated, he knew that much about her. Though she chose to work in a stable, Brody suspected that she'd probably never done a hard day's work in her life before arriving at the station. And there was the sense that Payton Harwell was the kind of woman who wouldn't give a guy like him a second glance out in the real world. She was seriously out of his league.

So why was she here, trying to seduce him? What did she really want from him beyond having a shag? Brody stood in front of her and cupped her cheek in his hand. Was it just an undeniable sexual attraction they shared? Or was it more?

He'd find some of his answers in her touch, in the feel of her body. And the rest, he'd leave for later. Spanning her waist with his hands, he pulled her body against his, then reached down and drew her leg up along his hip.

Her breath caught in her throat as he stared down into her eyes. Burying her fingers in his hair, she fixed her gaze on his mouth. "Well, then," she murmured, "I guess we're both ready now."

PAYTON ARCHED against the stable wall, reveling in the feel of Brody's hands on her body. It was so simple to want him. She didn't even think before falling into his arms. Maybe there was something in the water here in Australia. Or maybe it was just the man, Payton mused.

Something had changed inside her. For such a long time, she'd tiptoed through life, afraid to make a mistake, fearful that she might disappoint her parents. She'd been their only child, her difficult birth the cause of her mother's inability to have another baby. So there'd been a lot of pressure for her to be perfect.

But from the moment she'd hopped on that flight in Fiji, she'd felt a burden lift from her shoulders. Her parents would never forgive her, so there was no use trying to appease them. She could be whoever she wanted to be now. And she wanted to be wild and passionate, a woman who took chances and lived life.

She looked up into Brody's eyes. This was what she wanted, and not just his gorgeous face or his beautiful body, his penetrating gaze or his playful smile. He was what a real man was supposed to be—strong, confident and just a little bit dangerous. His muscles were hard and his hands rough.

Was that what she'd been looking for? Payton wondered. A man who had the power to possess her completely? Except for that very first time, she'd never made love outside the confines of a bedroom. But here she was, in a stable again, anxious to shed her clothes and feel him move inside her.

Here, everything seemed so much more real, more intense. She didn't feel sheltered and protected anymore. Instead, she'd become wild and uninhibited, like this land and the people around her, taking pleasure in the simplicity of everyday life—and everyday desires. This was her chance to start again. The ties to her past were gradually fraying.

Drawing a deep breath, Payton kissed him, this time making certain he understood her need. She slowly let her leg drop down along his hip, until she stood squarely in front of him. Then she tore at the buttons of his shirt.

He was as anxious as she was to get rid of the garment and a moment later, it lay on the straw at their feet. Payton ran her trembling hands from his shoulders to his belly and back up again. Then, she leaned forward and pressed a kiss to his warm skin, just below his shoulder.

What began gently gradually turned desperate. With every kiss, every caress, Payton wanted him more. He found the hem of her shirt and tugged it up, the fabric bunched in his fists as his hips pinned hers against the side of the stall. Slowly, Brody sank lower until his mouth was on her bare belly.

Payton's fingers furrowed through his hair and his lips trailed higher. He pulled at the lacy bra she wore and when his mouth captured her nipple, Payton cried out in surprise. A wave of sensation washed over her and for a moment, she wasn't sure she could stand.

Holding her tight, Brody tumbled them onto the blankets, pulling her on top of him. His fingers worked at the elastic that held her hair in check, freeing it to fall like a curtain around them both, and then he yanked her shirt over her head.

Payton sat up, straddling his hips, and ran her hand through her hair. Reaching behind her, she unhooked her bra and shrugged out of it. A tiny smile played at the corners of her mouth as she saw his expression shift.

"God, you are beautiful," he murmured, smoothing a hand over her shoulder to cup her breast. He rubbed her nipple to a hard peak and Payton closed her eyes. She didn't want to wait any longer. He could seduce her slowly some other time. Right now, she needed to satisfy a craving deep inside of her.

Payton pushed to her feet, standing over him, her gaze fixed on his. She kicked off her shoes, then slowly shimmied out of her jeans. There wasn't any hesitation or any insecurity. She knew exactly the effect she had on him.

She reached out for him and pulled him up beside

her. Her fingers worked at his belt and then his zipper and when he was standing in just his boxers, Payton let out a soft sigh. "That's better," she said.

He reached out and wrapped his arm around her waist, pulling her against his body. Brody's mouth came down on hers, his kiss deep and demanding. His hands skimmed over her. He knew exactly where to touch to make her ache with desire.

They fell back onto the blankets, Brody rolling her beneath him until his body was stretched out over hers, his hips cradled between her thighs. The delicious sensation of his weight sent a shiver through her limbs.

There were a lot of things Brody said that Payton didn't quite understand. They came from different worlds, and yet their desire for each other needed no translation. Her pulse racing, his hands searching, the anticipation growing between them until it was almost too much to bear.

As he moved above her, his shaft hard between them, Payton remembered her first time and the strange mix of fear and desire and excitement she'd felt. It was like that now with Brody, as if she were just a teenager, still in possession of her virginity.

She sensed this experience wouldn't be like anything she'd ever had before. He was different. But even more important, she was different. Something inside her had changed the moment she'd run away from her wedding. And it was time to see exactly what it was.

However, Brody seemed intent on taking his time. He smoothed his hands over her bare skin, sending shivers of sensation coursing through her body. His lips drifted lower until he drew her nipple into his mouth again.

Payton couldn't take it anymore. Holding him close, she rolled on top of him. Then she straddled his hips, feeling the hard ridge of his cock between them.

"We can do it that way, too." He grinned.

She reached for the condoms lying on the blanket next to them. His erection pressed out against the cotton fabric of his boxers, but she didn't take the time to pull them off. The need to feel him inside her had over-whelmed any thought of seduction.

After tugging the waistband down, she sheathed him, then drew her panties aside. A moment later, Payton slowly sank down on top of him, closing her eyes and holding her breath until he'd buried himself completely. She'd never taken control like this, but she knew exactly what she wanted and how it would feel.

Liberated, she thought as she slowly released her breath. Sex had always been an obligation with Sam, but now it was a basic need, a desire so strong that she'd lost any sense of propriety.

When she opened her eyes again, he was staring at her, passion burning in his gaze. "Don't move," he warned.

"I have to move," she replied with a slow smile. "That's the way it works. At least where I come from." She rose on her knees, then slowly lowered herself again.

"Oh, God, this is not going to last long if you can't follow directions."

Payton leaned forward and kissed him softly. "What is it they say? Just lie back and think of queen and country?"

Brody grabbed her hips and held her still. "Austra-lia is a constitutional democracy," he said.

"I don't care," Payton replied as she rocked forward, ignoring his plea. "We can discuss politics later."

What began slowly and purposefully soon dissolved into a frantic need to satisfy. Brody wasn't as close as he claimed and drove into her again and again, their bodies straining.

Payton felt the beginnings of her release grow inside her, the urge to surrender more intense than she'd ever experienced in the past. She closed her eyes and focused on the feel of him, the wonderful sensations that their coupling created in her body.

His hand touched her face and he drew her down again until their lips and tongues met. It was the kiss that sent her spiraling over the edge. The orgasm came as a complete surprise at first and then Payton was forced to let go, to surrender to the powerful shudders and spasms. She collapsed on top of him, and a moment later Brody found his own release, driving deep inside her, his body tense and then trembling.

They lay together for a long time, gasping for breath, neither one of them speaking. Payton wasn't sure what to say. Thanks were probably in order, considering she'd never experienced an orgasm so powerful. But then, this was only their first attempt. What would subsequent seductions bring?

"That's never happened before."

He gently pushed against her shoulders until their eyes could meet. "You're kidding, right?"

She felt a warm blush creep up her cheeks. If she was liberated enough to make love to a man she barely knew, then she should be able to express her desires. "I mean, it's happened, but not in that way."

He stared at her, a perplexed expression on his face. "Well, that's good, then."

"Yes," she said, smiling. "Maybe we could do it again?"

Brody chuckled. "I think we might have to wait just a bit."

"A bit? What is that in Australian? Because in American that means a minute at the most." She reached down and ran her fingers along his still-rigid shaft, pulling the condom off along the way.

Brody groaned as he clenched his teeth. "A minute. Maybe two." His breath caught in his throat. "Maybe less, if you're very gentle."

BRODY WASN'T SURE of the time. It was late. After midnight. He and Payton had chosen conversation over sex and she was curled up against him, her leg thrown over his hips and her cheek resting on his outstretched arm.

The batteries on the first torch had faded, but Brody had run out and gotten another. For now, they relaxed in complete darkness. Though he loved to look at her, he was just as content to communicate through touch. Her body was made for his hands, her skin so soft and her curves like a landscape to explore.

"We'd probably be more comfortable in my bed," he said, smoothing his hand over her tangled hair.

"We can't," she said.

"Why? There's nothing wrong with what we're doing."

"I know. I'm not ashamed. It's just…"

"What?"

"I'm an employee here and I should probably try to behave myself." She pushed up and grabbed the torch, then shined it on his face. "Besides, this is much more exciting, don't you think?"

"Exciting, maybe." Brody chuckled, holding up his hand. "But not nearly as comfortable." He rolled to his side and pulled a piece of straw from the blanket beneath him.

She sat up beside him and brushed her hair over her shoulder. With a lazy caress, she smoothed her hand over his belly. "When I saw you in the cell next to me, I thought about what you'd look like without your clothes."

Brody gasped, a laugh slipping from his lips. "Really?"

She nodded. "You look different than what I imagined."

"Different bad or different good?"

"Good," she said. Her fingers drifted lower, running along the length of his thigh. He watched, surprised at how such an innocent action could so easily stir his desire. He loved the feel of her hands on his body. As far as he was concerned, she could take whatever she wanted from him. He was willing and quite able to satisfy whatever need might arise.

Her fingers paused when she reached his knee and Brody sucked in a sharp breath. He knew it was ugly. The scars were still sharply defined, to the eye and to the touch. "What happened?" she asked.

He didn't want to tell the story again, especially not to her. It had been a foolish mistake that had changed the entire course of his life. But then, that course had led to her, hadn't it?

"I tore up my knee in a motorcycle accident," he said. "It's not nearly as bad as it looks. It happened a long time ago. I barely even think about it anymore." At least that was the truth, he mused.

She bent over him, her hair tickling his thigh, then pressed her lips to the scar. "There. All better."

Brody chuckled softly. "Yes. That does make things feel much better."

She pushed up on her hands and knees and crawled on top of him. In the soft light from the torch, Payton looked like some ancient goddess, her perfect skin gleaming like marble. He could imagine how a woman like her could drive men into battle for her favors. He was already lost and he'd only known her a few days.

"Any other interesting scars?"

"What exactly are you looking for? Defects?"

She picked up the torch again and shined the light on the tattoo on his right biceps. "What is this?" She rubbed her fingers over the inked skin.

"Nothing, really. Just something tribal."

"I have a tattoo," she said.

Brody pushed up on his elbow, stunned by the admission. "Where?"

She pointed to her ankle and he took the torch from her and held it there. "I don't see anything."

"There. It's that red dot right there."

"That's not a tattoo, that's a freckle."

"No, it was supposed to be a tattoo. But I chickened out after just a few seconds."

"Because it hurt?"

"No. Because I was afraid of what my parents might say. And my—" She smiled. "My boyfriend." She shook her head. "There were a lot of things I thought about doing and then never followed through on. Spontaneity was not something that was encouraged by my family."

"Tell me about this boyfriend," he said.

"That was a long time ago."

"What would they think of you now, lying here naked in a stable with me?"

"They'd probably have me committed."

Brody reached out and picked up her hand, then pressed it to his lips. "I wouldn't let them take you," he said. "You'd be safe with me."

A winsome smiled touched her lips. "I'm not sure *safe* is the right word."

Brody leaned forward and pulled her into a long, lingering kiss. "Will you spend the night with me?" he whispered.

"Here?"

"Wherever you want. Here is good."

"Gemma is probably going to wonder where I am."

"I think Callum is keeping her occupied," Brody assured her.

"The same way you're keeping me occupied?"

He shook his head. "I expect my brother has his own talents. He's—" Brody stopped short when a sound from outside the stall caught his attention. He reached over and switched off the torch, then pressed a finger to Payton's lips.

"What is it?" she whispered.

"Someone is out there."

The sound of horse's hooves on concrete echoed through the silence and Brody got to his feet and moved to the door of the stall. A moment later a light flicked on in the tack room, illuminating the interior of the stable enough to see who had intruded.

Payton stepped to his side, wrapped in one of the wool blankets, and peered out through the bars on the top edge of the stable door. "Who is it?"

"Teague," Brody whispered.

"What's he doing?"

"I think he's saddling his horse."

"Where is he going to ride in the dark?"

"Hell if I know," Brody said. He might guess where his brother was going. Hayley Fraser was back on Wallaroo Station. One plus one equaled two.

Brody thought about what Callum had said earlier. Family loyalty aside, whatever Teague was up to was his business and no one else's. Just like what went on between Payton and him didn't involve his brothers. They were adults now, and they made their own choices. "He's probably riding out to check on the herd," Brody said.

"Alone?"

"Yeah. Why not?"

They listened until the stable was once again silent, the light from the tack room left burning by his brother. Then Brody turned and tugged the blanket off of her. She squirmed playfully as he ran his free hand from her belly to her breast. "We're alone again," he said.

"We should get some sleep," Payton murmured.

Brody groaned as he kissed his way to her nipple. Teasing it to a peak with his tongue, he tried to convince her that sleep was the last thing on his mind. But when she ran her fingers through his hair and pulled his gaze up to hers, he realized just how tired she was. Her eyelids fluttered and she bit back a yawn.

"You're right," he said. "We both have to work tomorrow." Why the hell had he decided to bring her here? Brody wondered. If she hadn't taken this job, then they'd be free to do exactly what they wanted with their time. He should have bought them both a ticket to

Fremantle and they could have spent a week in his apartment. Or he could have found some private getaway where they'd be waited on hand and foot.

Instead, he'd brought her to the station, where they had to sneak around and hide in a horse stall to find some privacy. "You know, the weekend is coming up. You don't have to work on the weekend."

"What? Do you send the horses off to a spa on Saturday and Sunday?" she inquired with a raised brow. "They still need to be fed and groomed."

"But someone else can do that," Brody said.

"It's my job," she replied.

He drew a deep breath and sighed. "There has to be some benefit to sleeping with the owner's brother, don't you think?"

She slipped from his embrace and began to collect her clothes, scattered over the straw-covered floor. "There are a lot of benefits. But I'm not sure unlimited vacation time is one of them."

Brody wrapped his arms around her waist and pulled her back against him. "But aren't you interested in seeing some of Australia while you're here? Isn't that why you came? I'm sure Callum can get one of the jackaroos to take your job for a while."

She shook her head. "Not now. Maybe after I've worked here longer."

Brody understood her worry. After all, when he met her, she'd been reduced to petty crime just to survive. Here, she had a place to sleep, three meals a day and a paycheck at the end of each week. Security trumped great sex, at least for now.

"All right." He took Payton's clothes from her hands

and grudgingly helped her dress. Though she'd removed her clothes as quickly as possible, Brody didn't rush putting them back on, taking the chance to touch her one last time. When he finished, he pulled his jeans on, before slipping his bare feet into his boots. He didn't want to bother with the rest, tossing the remaining clothes over his arm.

"Come on, I'll walk you back to the bunkhouse."

Payton shook her head. "No. Wait here for a few minutes. I can walk back on my own." She pushed up onto her toes and gave him a sweet, lingering kiss. "I'll see you tomorrow," she whispered.

"Abso-bloody-lutely." He captured her mouth again with a deep and possessive kiss of his own.

"All right," she said, running her hands over his bare chest. "Tomorrow."

She turned and hurried out of the stable. Brody watched her as she disappeared into the dark. They'd only known each other for a few days, but he'd already twisted his life around hers. Living on the station had become almost tolerable and working the stock just a way to mark time until he could be with her again.

Brody knew the fascination would probably fade. It always had in the past with other women. There was something about Payton, though, that made him believe it might be different this time.

But was it her with her sweet smile and gentle touch? Or was it him? Had he finally let go of his former life and begun to look forward to what the future held?

4

A BEAD OF PERSPIRATION fell into Payton's eye and she straightened and brushed her arm over her damp forehead. Her back ached from the day's work—mucking out the stables and moving bales of straw into the freshly cleaned stalls. Setting the pitchfork against the rough wooden wall, she stretched her hands above her head and twisted to work the kinks out of her back.

"A dip in the hot tub would soothe those sore muscles," Teague said.

"Sounds good," Payton replied. "Maybe after dinner."

He stared at her for a long moment. "You know, you don't have to work quite so hard. Callum is already impressed. You do twice as much work as all of the jackaroos who've had the job before you."

"What exactly is a jackaroo?"

"Just another name for a stockman. Technically, you're a jillaroo since you're of the female variety."

She smiled. "I like that. I have a title. Maybe I should get some business cards printed. Payton Harwell, Jillaroo."

"Really, I'm serious. No one is going to fire you. And if you're trying to impress Brody, don't bother. He's never been one to enjoy station work."

"Why is that?"

Teague shrugged. "From the moment he could express an opinion, he wanted off the station. He's more like our mum than our dad. He finds it sheer drudgery."

"So, why does he stay?"

"I expect because you're here. Before you came, he spent most of his time in Bilbarra."

"No, I mean, why did he stay as an adult?"

"He didn't. He left the same time our mum did. Moved with her to Sydney when he was fourteen. After that, he only spent holidays here. He hasn't told you this?"

Payton shook her head. "We haven't really talked about our pasts. I guess we've been focusing on the present." She pulled off her gloves, then sat down on a nearby bale of straw. "So he's just here visiting?"

"He's been back for a while. Since his accident—"

"His motorcycle accident?"

Teague nodded. "Since his accident, he hasn't been able to play and he got dropped by his club."

"Club?"

"He hasn't told you much at all," Teague said. "Football club. He was a professional footballer. Aussie rules. He played for a club in Fremantle for the past five years. But he tore up his knee in the accident."

"I've seen the scar," she murmured. "He just brushed it off like it had happened years ago."

"He was in the hospital for a month and in a cast for six. He's lucky to be alive."

"I wonder why he didn't tell me?"

"He doesn't like to talk about it. The accident ended his career. Just when he was starting to play really well, too. And I suppose he thought it didn't make any difference." He sat down beside her. "Does it?"

"No. The scar doesn't bother me. Why would it? It's just that—" She shook her head.

"What?"

"I guess we don't know each other very well. At least not in that sense."

Teague shrugged. "Believe me, it isn't any easier when you know everything about each other. Maybe you and Brody are better off. Less…baggage?"

"Maybe." What Teague said might be true. She and Sam had known each other for years and the passion between them had faded to nothing more than a dull glow. But with Brody, there was fire, flames shooting up into the sky every time their bodies came together. Maybe all the things she didn't know just kept it more exciting.

"I'm flying into Brisbane day after tomorrow. Do you and Gemma want to ride along? You'd mentioned you wanted to shop."

"I have to work," she said.

"We'll be back before dark. I can't land on the station after sunset. And I'm sure some of the guys will take over your duties for a day."

"I don't have any money."

"Payday is Friday," Teague countered. "And I'd be happy to loan you a dollar or two if you're short."

"I couldn't ask you to do that."

"Hey, I think you're a trustworthy sort."

"Then you haven't heard of my criminal past," she said, laughing. "I met your bother in jail."

"Callum mentioned something about that. I guess we've all done things in the past that we wished we could change." He stood, then held out his hand to help her up. "Can I ask you something? From a woman's point of view?"

"Sure," she said.

"Do you think it's possible to forgive past mistakes? I mean, if things get royally stuffed up, is it possible to begin again?"

"I don't know," Payton said. She'd wondered the same thing. "I'm not sure you can ever go back and fix the mistakes you've made. You can just go forward and promise not to make them again."

He nodded, then smiled. "Yeah, I see what you mean." He drew a deep breath. "Listen, if it's all right with you, can we vaccinate those yearlings next week? I've got somewhere I need to be."

"I'm not going anywhere," she said. "Except to Brisbane, if you still plan to take us."

"That I do," he said as he strolled out of the stable. Brody passed him as he wandered in with his horse. Glancing back over his shoulder, he sent his brother an irritated frown, then turned to Payton. "What did he want?"

"He just stopped by to say hello," she said. "We were going to vaccinate the yearlings, but then something else came up." She slipped her gloves on. "He's going to fly Gemma and me to Brisbane on Saturday."

"And what are you and Gemma going to do in Brisbane?"

"Shop. I need to buy some work clothes," she said, glancing down at Davey's jeans and shirt. "And maybe we'll have some lunch and get a pedicure and a manicure. I'd like to get my hair cut, too. I feel like I need a change. This hair just gets in the way."

Brody rested his hands on her shoulders and dropped

a quick kiss on her lips. "But I like the way you look right now." He rubbed a stray strand between his fingers. "And I'm fond of your hair."

Pulling her against him, he kissed her again, this time more passionately. A shiver skittered through her body and she felt her desire warm. It didn't take much to make her want to pull him into a stall and tear off their clothes. "We could go to Brisbane together," he suggested. "Maybe spend the day at the beach instead. Do some surfing."

"It's really a girls' day out," she said. "I'm sure you can get along without me for a day, can't you?"

"I don't know," he teased.

"We'll spend the evening together. I'll be back before dark. Teague said he can't land once it's dark."

"Which means he'll probably find a way to keep you both in Brisbane for the night," he said cynically.

She shook her head. "I don't think so. I think Teague has something else going on."

"Why is that?"

"He asked my advice. Something about starting over again."

Brody sucked in a sharp breath. "Oh, hell. That can only mean one thing. Hayley Fraser. I figured that's where he was off to last night. Callum is going to be mad as a meat-ax."

A giggle slipped from Payton's lips.

"What?" Brody asked.

"How could a meat-ax get angry? And what is a meat-ax?"

"I don't know. What would you say?"

"Mad as a…wet hen?" She laughed. "All right. Yours is much better."

"Wet hen," he muttered. "That's just lame. Who would be afraid of a wet hen?"

"Why will Callum be angry?"

"There's a lot of history between our family and the Frasers. It has to do with a piece of land that Hayley's grandfather claims my great-grandfather stole from the Frasers. We've been fighting about it for years."

"A family feud. Like the Hatfields and McCoys." She paused. "The Montagues and Capulets."

"Yeah, I think Teague and Hayley fancied themselves Romeo and Juliet back when they were teenagers. They were obsessed with each other, to the point where my mum and dad thought they might run away and get married. Then Teague went off to university and a few months later, Hayley ran away. After that, he never mentioned her name again."

"What happened?"

Brody shrugged. "I don't know. Teague doesn't talk about it. He was really messed up for a while."

"So if they're Romeo and Juliet, who are we?" she asked. "Bonnie and Clyde?"

He grinned. "I loved that movie. And we did meet in jail."

"They died in the end of the movie. Riddled with bullets, I think."

"So you're expecting a happy ending for us? I can't think of a movie that ended happily. *Casablanca.* No, that one really didn't—how about—no, that one ended badly, too."

"Breakfast at Tiffany's," she murmured. A happy ending? Payton hadn't thought about the future at all. It was silly to think that she and Brody would share

anything beyond her time in Australia. "Life isn't a movie. It's not…perfect." She reached out and took the reins of his horse. "And I have work to do."

"Time for a break," he said. He circled her waist with his hands and lifted her until she could swing her leg over his horse, then handed her a small canvas bag. "Come on. Let's go for a ride."

Brody hooked his foot in the stirrup and settled behind her, taking the reins from her hands and slipping his arm around her waist.

"I haven't been on a horse in years," she said. "Where are we going?"

"I fancy a swim. And there's dinner in that sack."

"I don't have a suit."

"Then you can sit on the shore and watch for crocs."

He gave the horse a kick and guided it out of the stable. They rode in silence past the outbuildings and toward a small grove of trees in the distance. The sun was low in the late-afternoon sky but the air was still warm. Winter in Queensland was more like summer in Maine—the nights cool, sometimes chilly, and the days comfortably warm.

"Won't the water be cold?"

"The pond is pretty shallow," he said.

"Are there really alligators?"

"No. We don't have alligators, we don't have crocodiles, either. They're not common in this part of Queensland. Teague was just being cheeky with you." He paused. "Although, I suppose they could wander in here without us really knowing."

"Snakes, crocodiles, spiders. It's kind of easy to get hurt here."

He nuzzled his face into her neck. "I'll protect you."

"Who will protect you?"

They reached the pond a few minutes later. It wasn't like any pond Payton had ever seen. The water was brown, like the soil around it, and a pipe led from the pond to a nearby windmill. She studied the shoreline, searching for anything that moved. "How long can a crocodile hold its breath?"

"An hour, maybe more," Brody said. "The salt-water crocs are the bad ones. Freshwater crocs aren't nearly as nasty. And if they were here, they'd be on the shore, warming themselves in the sun."

He slid off the horse, then helped her down, before wrapping the reins around a nearby branch. Taking her hand, Brody led her to the edge of the water. Then he slowly began to remove his clothes.

"I really wish you wouldn't go in," she said.

"I've been swimming in this pond since I was a kid. Believe me, it's safe."

"And I think I'll just watch for a while," she said.

He kicked off his boots and socks, then slipped his jeans over his hips. A moment later, he was naked. Payton held her breath as she watched him walk to the water. He really was a beautiful man, every muscle in his body perfectly toned.

Desire raced through her body and her fingers clenched at the thought of touching him. Suddenly, crocodiles didn't seem like such a big deal. Not compared to swimming naked with Brody. As he sank into the water, Payton removed her jacket and dropped it to the ground. A moment later, she pulled off her shoes.

"My parents used to take me to the beach when we

went on vacation," she said. "And they'd never let me go in the water."

"Why not?"

"My mother was afraid of sharks. And my father was afraid I'd drown, even though I'd taken swimming lessons for years." Payton shook her head. "They spent so much energy protecting me from alligators that weren't there."

"Crocodiles," he said.

When she skimmed her jeans down over her thighs, he smiled. And when she was left in just her underwear, he slowly stood. She walked to the water's edge. "Take it all off," he said softly.

Payton drew a ragged breath. They'd been naked together last night, in the shadows of the stable. But it felt just a little bit naughty out in the open. Still, her desire for him was strange and powerful, a force she didn't want to deny.

The water was cold on her skin and she groaned as it slowly moved up her body. Then, holding her breath, she slipped beneath the surface and popped up in front of him. "It's freezing!" she cried.

He pulled her into his arms. "You'll be warm soon," he said, letting his hands drift over her body.

"I've never done this before. I've always thought it would be fun to swim naked, but I've never had the opportunity." As he wrapped her legs around his hips, she leaned back, letting her hair fan out in the water. "It feels nice on my sore muscles."

"You work too hard."

"That's what Teague was telling me," she said as she floated on the surface of the pond.

"And what else was Teague telling you?" Brody asked, an edge to his inquiry.

"Nothing." She didn't want to tell Brody that she'd had an interesting conversation with his older brother, that he'd told her things Brody hadn't bothered to mention. Even now, as she looked into his eyes, Payton saw him differently.

He wasn't just an object of her desire anymore. He was a man with a real life, a life that hadn't gone exactly as planned. But then, her life wasn't exactly a fairy-tale, either. Payton smiled.

She felt his eyes on her naked body and a moment later his hands smoothed over her breasts and down her belly. The sensation was like nothing she'd ever felt before. His touch was warm yet cold, fleeting yet so stirring. Every sensation seemed magnified by the water, her skin slick and prickled with goose bumps.

When he touched her between the legs, a tiny moan slipped from her throat. His caress was so light, so skilled that Payton felt the rise of her need almost immediately. Her eyes still closed, she gave herself over to the feeling. The water lapped around her body, her skin chilly in the late-afternoon air.

She still couldn't understand how easy it was with Brody. She wanted him and he wanted her. They satisfied each other in the most basic way, driven purely by sexual desire. And yet, there was an intimacy growing between them, a trust that seemed strengthened by their passion.

He slipped a finger inside her and she felt herself losing control. And then, a heartbeat later, Payton dissolved into spasms of pleasure. She arched back as the orgasm rocked her body and for a moment, she sank beneath the surface.

But then Brody grabbed her and pulled her up against his chest. Payton coughed and sputtered. She wrapped her arms around his neck, her heart slamming. Another shudder shook her body and he held her tight.

"Are you all right?" Brody asked, brushing the wet hair away from her face.

She nodded, wiping the water from her eyes. Then she began to giggle and couldn't seem to stop. The things Brody did to her were scandalous—she felt wicked when she was with him. Payton kissed him hard. "I think you're more dangerous than the crocodiles. But what a wonderful way to go."

THERE WERE TIMES—though not many—when Brody truly did appreciate the beauty of the outback. He stared up at the inky-black sky, picking out the constellations that he recognized as the moon slowly rose. "Look," he said, pointing to a shooting star. "Quick, make a wish." He drew Payton closer, his arm wrapped around her shoulders. "Got it?"

She nodded as she lay beside him on his bedroll. "The stars are different here."

He pointed into the darkness. "There's the Southern Cross. And the Milky Way."

"No Big Dipper. Or Orion."

"We have Orion," he said. "In the summer. Orion is upside down here. Standing on his head." He rolled onto his side to face her. "It's not much, but it's all the station has to offer for entertainment."

"The swim and the sunset and the stars were perfect," Payton said softly.

"Better than all those balls and cotillions you used to go to?"

"Much better," she said, turning to face him. "And I didn't go to that many balls. Well, maybe I did. But my mother was into those kinds of things. High society and all that. Her one goal in life was to find me a good husband."

"And now you're here in low society with me."

She shook her head. "I'm exactly where I want to be."

"And how long will you be here?" Brody asked, twirling a strand of her hair around his finger.

"I hadn't thought about it. I came in on a tourist visa, so I have three months." She shook her head. "I like it here. I'm not leaving anytime soon."

He drew a deep breath. "Don't you think about going home? To your family and friends?"

She turned her attention back to the stars and Brody sensed she was avoiding his question. She seemed to be reluctant to talk about what had brought her to Oz. He suspected she wasn't just a student touring the country. If she came from a wealthy family, what was she doing working for slave wages on a cattle station? And why had she run out of money so quickly?

"You don't belong here," he said.

"I don't have anyplace else to be right now," Payton replied.

"I don't believe that. What are you running away from, Payton?"

"Nothing," she said. She glanced over at him. "Really. Nothing."

"Talk to me," Brody said, suddenly desperate to know more. Sooner or later, the sex wouldn't be enough. And if there was nothing else to hold her here, to keep her in Australia, she'd leave.

"There's nothing to say," she insisted. "And what difference does it make, anyway?"

He'd always been realistic about his relationships with women. He'd been an enthusiastic lover, romantic when the time called for it, and supportive if required. But he'd never surrendered his heart, never allowed himself to get too close.

Yet the intimacies he'd shared with Payton made him want more. He needed to know who she was and where she came from. He longed to know how she felt about him. Why was she here and how long would she stay? "Fine," he muttered. "And I suppose I shouldn't be surprised if I wake up one day and you've just moved on."

"I wouldn't do that," she said. "I'd say goodbye."

"Well, that's nice to know." Brody couldn't keep the sarcasm from his tone. He pushed to his feet and walked over to the edge of the pond, the moonlight gleaming on the water. He grabbed a small pebble and threw it into the pond, hearing the *plunk* before the ripples glimmered in the dark.

He closed his eyes when he felt her hand on his back. "I don't understand what you want," she said.

"I don't know what I want." He turned and pulled her into his embrace. How could he answer that? All he knew was he didn't want to hold anything back. He wanted honesty and openness and complete surrender. But then, he hadn't been honest with her. Perhaps that's where it would have to start.

The problem with his story was it really didn't make him look good. He hadn't planned well for his future, he'd bet everything on a successful football career. And then, in one incredible act of stupidity, he'd blown it all.

"We should go back," he said. "It's starting to get really cold and I don't want to you catch a chill."

He rolled up his swag and retied it onto the back of his saddle, then took her hand and led her over to his horse.

She looked up at him and forced a smile. "Thank you for bringing me here. It was fun."

Grasping her waist, Brody helped her up into the saddle. After he mounted, he turned the horse toward the house. Payton leaned back against him and he turned his face into her damp hair, inhaling her scent.

"Stay with me," he said.

"I'm not going to leave."

"I mean tonight. Stay with me tonight."

"Not tonight," she said.

"I want you with me," he said. "I don't like sneaking around. We're not doing anything wrong, why do you act as if we are?"

"Because it's just between us right now," she said. "Nothing can mess it up if it's just us. I've known you for three days, Brody. We should at least try to take a few things slowly, don't you think?"

This was exactly why he couldn't be friends with a woman. He didn't understand the reasoning. It was all right to have sex in the stable, but not in his bed. Everyone on the station knew what was going on between them, but pretending that nothing was happening made more sense.

Arguing with her wouldn't help, he mused. If he

wanted more from her, then he'd just have to wait until she was ready to give him more. When they reached the bunkhouse, he helped her down and gave her a quick kiss. "I'll see you tomorrow," he murmured.

She nodded. "Tomorrow."

He turned away and led his horse toward the stable. As he passed by the house, he saw Callum sitting on the back porch, a beer in his hand, his feet kicked up on the railing. "Where were you?" Callum asked.

"I went for a swim with Payton," Brody said. He swung off his horse and wrapped the reins around the post at the bottom of the steps. "Do you have another one of those?"

Callum reached down and picked up a bottle. "You have to go fetch the next round," he said.

Brody twisted off the cap, then sat down in the chair beside Callum's. He took a long drink of the beer and belched.

"Nice," Callum said. "A bit more choke and you would have started."

"Thank you," Brody muttered.

"Funny how you're on your best behavior around Payton and then you revert to typical Brody."

"And you don't put on airs when you're with Gemma?" He paused. "And why aren't you with Gemma? How come you're all alone here, crying into your beer?"

"She's shut herself in the library. I can't understand what's taking her all this time. It's not like we're royalty. But she's going over every single journal and account book in there."

"What does that have to do with our family history?"

"Don't ask me," Callum said.

"She's pretty. Not as pretty as Payton, but pretty."

"I beg to differ," Callum said. "Gemma is much prettier."

"Payton told me she spoke with Teague today. He was talking like he'd started things up with Hayley Fraser again. And he took off in the middle of the night last night on horseback."

"Shit," Callum said. "When I heard she was back, I wondered if he was going to see her again. What do you think she's up to?"

"You never liked her, did you?"

Callum shrugged. "She put Teague through hell the first time they were together. He has a blind spot when it comes to her."

"Maybe that's our problem," Brody mused. "We've never had a blind spot when it comes to a woman. Maybe we're missing out on something."

Callum took a drink of his beer. "Maybe." He pulled his feet off the railing and stood. "I'm going to go check on Gemma. See if she might need some help." He stepped over Brody's outstretched legs and walked back inside the house.

Brody glanced over at the light shining from the window of the bunkhouse. If Gemma was in the library then that meant Payton was alone in the bunkhouse. He drank the last of his beer as he wandered off the porch toward the light.

When he rapped on the door, there was no answer from inside, but he heard the sound of running water and walked around the corner of the bunkhouse to the rough wooden shower. He pulled the door open and stepped inside, slipping his hands around Payton's waist.

She screamed, but he stopped the sound with his kiss, his tongue delving into her damp mouth until her surprise was subdued.

She brushed her soapy hair from her eyes and looked at him. "Your clothes are getting all wet," she said.

His fingers skimmed over her naked body, deliberately tempting her. "I just wanted to say good-night." He leaned forward, his lips barely touching hers.

"I thought you did that already," Payton said.

"I wanted to leave you with something a bit more memorable," he said. His hands slid around to cup her backside and he pulled her hips against his, making his desire completely evident.

Brody's mouth found Payton's again and he felt her melt against him. "If you want more, I'm in the first room at the top of the stairs." With that, Brody stepped out of the shower. "Good night, Payton. Sleep tight."

She didn't return the courtesy. He imagined that she was considering his offer. But Brody really didn't expect her to follow through. Not tonight. But maybe tomorrow night. A grin curved the corners of his mouth. He could be bloody persuasive when he wanted.

THOUGH SHE WAS EXHAUSTED, Payton couldn't sleep. Her head spun with thoughts of Brody. She wanted to go to him, to crawl into his bed and into his arms and just fall asleep with him beside her. The need was so acute it had become an ache.

Cursing softly, she tossed aside the bedcovers and swung her legs off the edge of the bunk. Gemma had come in an hour before and Payton had assumed she was asleep, but then she spoke.

"Can't sleep?" she called from across the room.

"No. You can't, either?"

"No."

A moment later, the light on Gemma's headboard came on. She sat up, crossing her legs in front of her, then ran her hand through her thick auburn hair. "Would you care to talk?" she asked. "I'm a good listener. All my friends tell me so."

"It's complicated," Payton replied.

"I can handle complicated. Is it Brody? You two seem to be…attracted."

"That's putting it mildly," Payton said. She crawled out of bed and crossed the room, then sat down on the edge of Gemma's bunk. "Can you keep a secret?"

"Of course."

"A month ago this last Saturday, I was putting on my wedding gown in Fiji and getting ready to walk across the beach and get married."

Gemma gasped. "Oh, goodness. What happened?"

"I got scared and ran away." She frowned, searching for the words to explain her actions. "I just wasn't sure he was the man I wanted to spend the rest of my life with. There was no…fire. Do you know what I mean?"

Gemma nodded. "Yes," she said. "I know precisely what you mean."

"So I grabbed a few things, stuffed them in my bag, exchanged my honeymoon ticket for a flight to Brisbane and…disappeared into the outback."

"And here you are," Gemma said.

"Yes."

"Have you called your family?"

Payton shook her head. "I left a message at the hotel

in Fiji after I landed in Australia. I said I'd call them soon, but they're going to be so angry with me that I don't even want to think about that now. The embarrassment and the expense of the wedding. The gossip will be awful."

"What of your fiancé?"

"I can't imagine what he's thinking. I'm sure he doesn't want anything more to do with me. Not that I want him to. I made my choice and I can live with it."

"Well, there it is, then," Gemma said cheerfully. "As Callum would say, no worries."

"Oh, I have plenty to worry about. Like this thing with Brody. I'm sure it's just a reaction to what I did. I was a little…repressed and now I'm testing my boundaries. And the attraction will probably fade soon. But then, I'm not sure I want it to." Payton paused. "He's like a rebound guy, but I think he might be more."

"A rebound guy?" Gemma said. "I understand. But wouldn't any man who came after your fiancé be a rebound guy? So, in theory, it would be better to go out with some git after you break up so you don't waste a good bloke as a rebound guy."

"I suppose that would be sensible. So you think I'm wasting Brody?"

"Or perhaps, you could consider the possibility that fate has put this man in your path and the reason you ran away from your wedding is that you were really meant to be with him all along."

"No," Payton said, the notion too absurd to consider. "You think so?"

"I think it's silly to try to figure out a relationship before it's really begun. Maybe you should just let it happen."

Payton considered Gemma's point, then slowly

stood. "Thank you," she said. She walked over to her bunk and grabbed her jacket from where it hung on the bedpost. "I'm just going to visit Brody for a few minutes. Don't wait up for me."

"I won't," Gemma said with a sly smile.

Payton slipped her shoes on and pulled the jacket over her T-shirt and flannel pajama bottoms. The night was chilly as she ran from the bunkhouse to the main house. Mary had left a light burning over the sink in the kitchen, but the house was silent. Tiptoeing through the kitchen, she headed toward the stairs. But when she reached the top, she was faced with two choices.

Brody had said his bedroom was the first door at the top of the stairs, but she couldn't remember if he'd said on the right or the left. She reached for the door on the right and opened it carefully. To her relief, she found a linen closet stacked with towels.

Drawing a deep breath, she opened the opposite door and slipped inside. The bedside lamp still burned and Brody's hand rested on a sports magazine that he had been reading before he fell asleep. He slept in a tangle of blankets, his chest bare and his hair tousled.

Payton slowly undressed, dropping her clothes on the floor. When she was naked, she stepped to the side of the bed and gently moved the magazine from beneath his hand. He looked so relaxed, almost boyish. His brow, usually furrowed into an intense expression, was now smooth, and his lips, so perfectly sculpted, were parted slightly.

Payton carefully pulled the covers back and slipped into bed beside him. He awoke with a start and stared at her for a long moment before he comprehended what was going on. Then, with a soft sigh, he rolled her beneath him and kissed her.

There was no need for words. They communicated with taste and touch, with soft moans and quickened breathing. Payton slid her hand down and wrapped her fingers around his rigid cock and at the same moment, he found the damp spot between her legs.

All the while, as they teased each other closer to the edge, he kissed her gently, murmuring her name and telling her how good it felt to touch her. At first, Payton was a bit inhibited talking about such things. But then, she let her insecurities go and began to take part in the highly charged conversation.

She could feel his body tense as she brought him closer, his breath coming in short gasps. Carefully, Payton drew him back from the edge, becoming more skillful with every caress. Brody took his cues from her and did the same until they were both almost frantic for release, writhing against each other, their limbs tangled in the sheets.

And when her need finally overwhelmed her, Payton knew that it was exactly what she was searching for. He surrendered a moment later, her hand becoming slick with his orgasm.

Brody's mouth found hers and he kissed her gently. Such a simple thing, Payton mused. And yet, every time they surrendered to each other, she felt the bond between them growing. It wasn't just sex. They were discovering each other and with each new experience, Payton found herself wanting more.

"Are you going to stay?" he asked, his lips brushing against hers as he spoke.

Payton nodded. It would be easy enough to sneak out before morning. But then, why even bother to deny what was happening between them? They were both free to enjoy each other. They were both consenting adults. Any shame she might have felt about sleeping with a man she barely knew was just residual guilt left over from leading a rather sheltered life.

She wasn't the same Payton who had flown to Fiji for her wedding. She wasn't even the same Payton who had run away in the middle of the ceremony. Every day she was on her own, she was learning more and more about the woman she really was inside.

She'd spent so much time in familiar surroundings, safe among family and friends, her every need met, her every worry soothed, that she hadn't really bothered to question who she was or what she wanted. But now, each day was a choice, a choice to go backward or to move forward.

"You're not a dream, are you?" Brody whispered, running his fingers through her hair.

"No," she said.

"You won't be gone the next time I open my eyes?"

"No."

Satisfied, Brody pulled her against his body, tucking her backside into his lap and wrapping his arms around her. His lips pressed to her nape and Payton closed her eyes, a warm feeling of contentment washing over her.

The world she'd once known seemed like another lifetime. She was happy here in Brody's arms. And whether it lasted a day or a year, she wouldn't question it again, for perhaps Gemma had been right. Perhaps fate had brought them together.

5

BRODY PARKED the Land Rover in front of Shelly's coffeeshop, waiting for the dust on Bilbarra's main street to settle before stepping out of the truck. He had just enough time for a late lunch before heading back to the station.

Gemma and Payton had taken off with Teague at sunrise for their girls' day out in Brisbane. To keep his mind off Payton, Brody had driven into Bilbarra to pick up a part for one of the windmills that had gone down the previous week.

But the long ride in had left him plenty of time to think about the past five days. It had only been five days since he'd first set eyes on Payton. Hard to believe considering what had passed between them. It wasn't just the desire, Brody thought. He'd felt that way about other women, at least in the beginning. But he found himself focused on different matters when it came to Payton—like how long she'd stay and whether she had any reason to go home.

They seemed to fit so perfectly, understanding each other's needs without even having to speak, focusing on the present instead of the future. He needed a woman like that, a woman who wouldn't insist on plans and promises.

She'd spent the last three nights in his bed, though she hadn't been brave enough to face the group at the breakfast table. Instead, she'd slipped out in the hour before dawn, while the house still slept.

Oddly enough, his brothers wouldn't have even noticed her comings and goings. Teague hadn't bothered to come home the past two nights, only just turning up to grab a shower and change clothes. And Callum had his own preoccupations, disappearing with Gemma the night before last and returning the next morning.

It was strange that all three of them were suddenly involved when not one of them had bothered with dating for months. He headed toward the post office, but a shout stopped him in the middle of the street.

"Brody Quinn!"

Brody turned to see Angus Embley lumbering after him, his tie undone and his hair standing on end.

"I haven't done anything wrong," Brody said, holding up his hands in mock surrender.

"I've been wanting to speak with you," Angus said. He motioned Brody toward police headquarters and Brody jogged across the street, joining him on the porch. "Why have you been dodging my calls?"

"I'm sorry," Brody said. "I was just planning to go over to the Spotted Dog and pay Buddy for that mirror I broke last weekend."

"I'm not worried about Buddy's damn mirror. I'm on the organizing committee for Bachelors and Spinsters and we're going to hold an auction this year. You're the only celebrity we've got in Bilbarra besides Hayley Fraser and I don't think we can convince her to participate. You'd fetch a pretty penny. All the proceeds go to the library book fund. And you don't have to sleep with anyone, just have dinner together."

Though every unmarried person within a two-hundred-mile radius looked forward to the annual Bilbarra "ball," Brody and his brothers suddenly had three very good reasons not to attend—Payton, Gemma and Hayley. "I heard Hayley was back on Wallaroo Station," Brody mentioned, hoping for some additional news.

Angus looked surprised. "Really." He appeared to weigh his options for a moment, then shook his head. "Naw. She's a big telly star. She's probably got a whole building full of people telling her what she can and can't do."

"I think I'm going to have to pass," Brody said.

"Hey, there is something else." Angus braced his arm on the porch post. "There's a private detective hanging about."

"Looking for me?"

Angus chuckled. "One would think that might be a good bet. But he's looking for that lady you bailed out of my jail. Payton Harwell. What did you do with her after you bailed her out?"

Brody considered his answer for a long moment. He could trust Angus, but the man was an officer of the law. If Payton was a fugitive, Angus might not have a choice in taking sides. Brody shrugged. "I gave her some money and sent her on her way. She said she was headed back to Brisbane. That's the last I saw of her."

Angus frowned. "There's a reward for information. Ten thousand American."

"What did she do?"

"He wouldn't say. You could ask him yourself. He was looking to have a bit of lunch, so I pointed him toward the coffeeshop. He may still be there."

"Thanks," Brody said, starting off down the street.

Hell, this was all he needed. He was lucky he hadn't brought Payton to town with him. He'd been concerned about her flying to Brisbane with Teague, but she seemed almost anxious to get off the station and spend time shopping with Gemma. The testosterone-heavy atmosphere on the station did require time away occasionally.

If she was running from something—or someone—then who could say when she'd just up and disappear again? Maybe she planned to use the trip to Brisbane to make her escape. He shook his head. She'd promised to say goodbye before she left. He'd have to take her at her word.

The bell above the door of the coffeeshop jingled as he stepped inside. "Hey there, Shelly!" Brody slid onto one of the stools at the counter and picked up a menu.

Shelly Farris wiped her hands on a towel and strolled over to him. "Brody Quinn. What brings you into town on a weekday?"

Brody set the menu down and watched as she poured him a cup. "I'm picking up a few parts for Callum. I thought I'd check up on you. See if you made any of my favorite meat pies today."

"We have steak mince, steak and mushroom, and a few of our breakfast pies left."

"I'll have a steak mince," Brody said. "Make them takeaway." He closed the menu and glanced over his shoulder. There was only one other customer in the place. "Tourist?" he asked, nodding in the man's direction.

Shelly shook her head. "No. Private investigator. Looking for that girl who stiffed me on the bill last week. The bill you paid. I don't think you did society any favors there."

"Why? What did he tell you?"

"Nothing. Only that he's offering a reward for information. I couldn't give him more than what I just told you. Do you know where she is?"

Brody shook his head. "No, how would I? I was just doing a good deed."

Shelly disappeared into the kitchen to get his order while Brody sipped his coffee. If he wanted to know more about Payton Harwell, all he had to do was ask. But by asking, he might create undue suspicion. Still, idle curiosity wasn't out of the ordinary.

He slipped off the stool and wandered over to the booth where the middle-aged man sat, a half-eaten Lamington on his plate. "Don't like the dessert?" Brody asked.

The man glanced up from the study of his mobile phone. "What?" He looked at his plate and smiled. "No. It was great. Can I get my check?"

"I don't work here," Brody said.

"Oh, sorry."

When the man made a move to leave, Brody sat down on the opposite side of the booth. "I hear you're looking for someone."

"Yes. Yes, I am." He reached into a leather folder and pulled out a photo, then set it down in front of Brody. "Do you know her?"

Brody nodded. "I do. We were incarcerated together."

His eyebrow shot up. "I knew she spent some time in the local jail, but I didn't know you were with her when she was arrested."

"I wasn't," Brody said. "We just happened to be confined at the same time. I paid her fine and settled her accounts. Why are you looking for her?"

"It's a private matter," he said. "Do you know where she is?"

"Did she break the law?"

"As I said, it's a private matter. But there is a reward for information leading to her location, if you know something."

"I bailed her out and then dropped her on the road out of town. I think she said she was going to make her way down to Sydney," Brody lied. "I told her she could probably catch a ride on one of the road trains that pass through."

"Road trains?"

"It's a semitruck that pulls a string of trailers. They pass through Bilbarra occasionally, hauling feed and building supplies." He leaned back and stretched his arms out to rest on the edge of the bench. "She could be anywhere by now."

"Yes, well, thank you," the man said. "That's the most I've found to go on. She didn't say anything about where she might be staying or whether she met up with any friends?"

Brody pretended to ponder the question for a moment, then shook his head. "Nope. She just wanted to get out of town."

The investigator threw a wad of cash onto the table, then held out his hand. "Your lunch is on me," he said. "Thanks for the information."

"No worries," Brody said. "I hope you find her." He watched as the man walked out the front door then went back to his spot at the counter. When Shelly returned with his meat pies, he pointed to the empty booth. "He's buying me lunch."

"Well, there's a clever boy. What did you tell him?"

Brody scooped up the pies wrapped in paper, and took a big bite out of one of them. "Not much," he said as he chewed. "But I got a free lunch out of it." He headed toward the door.

"Where are you going?" Shelly asked, disappointment tingeing her tone. "I just rang my husband to stop by. Arnie's got himself mixed up in some silly football scheme with the boys over at the Spotted Dog and he needs advice on his footy picks. He's been losing twenty dollars a week to those fools."

"I'm out of the game," Brody said, pointing to his knee. "I'm trying my best to forget footy."

"You were one of the best, Brody Quinn," Shelly called.

As Brody strode down the street, he inhaled the two meat pies. He was tempted to stop by the Spotted Dog for a beer to wash them down, then realized he'd been banished from the place until further notice. Instead, he decided to stop at the local library. A quick Internet search might turn up a few clues on Payton and her past…and maybe even outline her crimes.

The public library was attached to the small school in Bilbarra. Though nearly all of the children who lived on cattle and sheep stations took their classes by computer, those who lived within a short drive of Bilbarra attended a regular school. Some of the advanced classes were still taught online, but there were two teachers that guided the thirty or forty students through their studies, and the town librarian to see to their literary needs.

When he walked into the library, a trio of young boys gathered at a large table. One of the boys recognized him immediately and quickly informed his friends. The librarian, Mrs. Willey, looked up at the commotion, then smiled. "See there," she said. "Everyone uses the library, even football legends."

Brody grinned. "She's right, you know. The library is one of my favorite spots in all the world. Read more books!" He stopped at the counter. "There," he muttered. "I've done my duty as a role model, ma'am. Now, I was wondering if I could use a computer with Internet access."

"Certainly," Mrs. Willey said. "Use any one of those three along the wall. But I'll have you know, accessing adult material is prohibited and will result in the suspension of your privileges."

He caught her teasing smile and chuckled. "There'll be none of that," he said. "I'm here to look up some recipes."

He sat down and keyed in his favorite search engine then typed Payton's first and last name. Brody paused before he hit Enter, wondering what he'd find. Maybe it would be something he didn't like, something he'd rather not know. And shouldn't he wait for Payton to tell him about her past? Real relationships were supposed to be about trust.

He had to know all the facts before he could protect

her, Brody rationalized. If she was in trouble, he'd do everything in his power to help her. "So I have to know," he said as he hit the keys.

"Payton Harwell," he read. "Over one thousand hits?" Brody clicked on the first one and found her name mentioned as the winner of a horse show. But right below that was a startling headline: Payton Harwell to Wed Heir to Whitman Fortune.

He clicked on the article and an instant later, a photo of Payton and her fiancé appeared. He scanned through the text beneath it and stopped at the wedding date. "The couple will be married on the island of Fiji in late April with close friends and relatives in attendance. The bride will wear a gown by designer Sophia Carone."

Late April? If Payton had been married in late April and he'd met her the first of June, then her marriage hadn't lasted more than a month. "Oh, shit," Brody muttered. Had he been having a naughty on a nightly basis with a married woman?

There weren't many rules in Brody's book when it came to sex, but not bedding another man's wife was one of them. After witnessing the problems in his parents' marriage, he'd vowed never to be involved in breaking up a family. Besides, there had always been plenty of single women willing to jump into bed with him, he'd had no need to do it with the married sort.

He leaned back in his chair and studied the photo. They looked happy, their arms wrapped around each other, smiling for the photographer. Worse, they looked as if they belonged together, living in some fancy mansion in New York with servants to tend to their every need.

Well, at least she wasn't a criminal, Brody mused. She was simply a runaway wife. He paused. Or maybe a runaway bride. There was no proof that she'd ever gone through with the wedding. Maybe she'd arrived in Fiji and decided marriage just wasn't for her.

"Is there anything I can help you with?"

Brody quickly clicked back to the search engine, then glanced over his shoulder at Mrs. Willey. "No. Nothing. Just catching up on a few of my old friends." He stood, shoving his hands into the pockets of his jeans. "Thanks. I'm in a bit of a hurry right now, but I'll stop by soon and pick up some books."

"You do that," she said with a wide smile. "Be sure to come on a school day if you can. I'm sure the students would love to talk to you."

Brody strode out the front door of the library into the midday sun. He headed back to the Land Rover, parked near the coffeeshop. He'd have to decide just how to discuss his discovery with Payton. Though his rule regarding married women still stood, it seemed rather pointless to avoid sex now that that horse was already out of the barn.

Hell, the only way to avoid wanting her was to leave Queensland altogether. He could no more control his desire for Payton Harwell than he could stop breathing.

THE PLANE TOUCHED DOWN as the afternoon sun hovered near the western horizon. Payton peered out the window, catching sight of one of the station's utes, the name she'd learned to call the pick-up trucks that nearly everyone drove. She saw Callum leaning against the truck as the plane taxied to the near end of the runway, but Brody was nowhere to be seen.

When Teague had turned off the single engine, Callum approached and opened the door. He helped Payton out, grabbing shopping bags as she jumped lightly from the plane. He then turned back to wrap his hands around Gemma's waist. Payton watched as their gazes met and he gave her a quick kiss.

Though Gemma hadn't said anything about her relationship with the eldest Quinn, it was clear to everyone that something was going on. Callum didn't smile much, but he always seemed to be smiling when Gemma was present.

Callum helped Teague secure the plane before all four of them hopped into the truck and headed toward the house. Payton had hoped to find Brody standing on the porch or lounging on her bunk, but she was disappointed.

"He took off about a half hour ago," Callum said. "On horseback, toward the west. I'm sure he'll be back soon."

Payton forced a smile. She'd been looking forward to seeing Brody all day. She'd bought a sexy new swimsuit for the hot tub and some lacy underwear that she was certain he'd appreciate. Her nails and toes looked perfect and her hair smelled like fruit. In short, she was almost irresistible.

She set her bags inside the door of the bunkhouse then turned and jogged down the front steps. "I'm going to ride out and meet him," she said.

"It's getting dark," Callum warned.

"Don't worry, I won't go far. I can see the lights of the station from pretty far away."

She ran to the stables and found a gentle mount, then quickly saddled the horse. She tied a bedroll on the back in case she and Brody decided to make a stop at the swimming hole again. Then, after swinging her leg over the saddle, she steered the horse out of the stable and into the waning light.

Though she'd ridden to the pond with Brody the other night, this was the first time she'd been on a horse alone since her fall nine years before. "Like riding a bike," she said, settling into the rhythm.

She urged the horse into a relaxed gallop, letting the wind whip her hair into a riot of curls. It was still easy to see where she was going, the last rays of the sun shining on the red dirt of the outback.

As she rode, her thoughts wandered to Brody, to spending the evening alone with him. Brisbane had been so busy and exciting that she'd wished he'd been there to share it with her. Maybe next weekend they could go together, as he'd suggested. They could spend some time at the beach or find a comfy hotel room and revel in absolute privacy.

As the sun dropped lower, the air became chilly and Payton drew her horse to a stop. She scanned the landscape for Brody, but it was difficult to see. Tugging gently on the reins, she turned the horse around. Her breath caught in her throat. She couldn't see the station anymore.

Rubbing her eyes, she squinted into the distance, searching for the lights that would guide her back. Slowly, she realized she'd ridden too far, lost in her thoughts and unaware of the passing time. Everything looked the same. Starting off in the direction she'd come from, Payton kicked the horse into a gallop again.

But a moment later, the horse stumbled in an unseen gully and she found herself thrown forward.

Payton hit the ground with a hard thud, knocking the wind out of her. Groaning, she lay back in the dirt and took a quick inventory. Her limbs were still intact, no broken bones, just wounded pride. Levering to her feet, she brushed the dirt off her jeans and remounted, but as soon as she spurred the horse forward, she could feel the animal favor its right foreleg.

Sliding off again, she bent down and ran her hands over his leg. "What happened?" she cooed. There was no swelling and no broken bones. She's seen enough stumbles in her show-jumping career to suspect that it was probably just a bruise. Though riding was possible, there was no need to put the horse under any more stress. She mentally calculated the distance and figured she probably had at least an hour's walk.

Payton stared up at the stars, trying to remember what she'd seen in the night sky. The last traces of the day were visible on the horizon, so she grasped the reins and began to walk the opposite way, east, toward the station.

The outback looked deceptively flat, yet as she walked, she realized that a gentle rise could easily hide things in the distance. She tried to keep moving in a straight line, finding a cluster of stars to keep over her right shoulder. But it was difficult to maintain her bearings in the dark. In the end, she decided to give her horse its head. He knew how to get home better than she did.

But, to her surprise, the horse didn't lead her back to the station. Instead, she found herself standing at a low iron gate. She hadn't come through any fence on her way out, but the horse seemed to know what it was doing. "Do I trust the horse or do I trust myself?"

In the end, she opened the gate and led the horse through. A few seconds later, she noticed the outline of a small building, just barely visible in the growing moonlight. Obviously, the horse had been to the spot in the recent past. "What is this?"

The front door was unlocked, but she could see nothing in the black interior. Closing her eyes, she felt around with her hands, stumbling over what felt like beds along the walls. She wandered back to the porch, then noticed a lantern hanging beside the door and a tin box of matches nailed below it.

The match flared and she lit the lantern, then walked back into the small shack. It was obvious it was some kind of remote bunkhouse, though it seemed to be awfully close to Kerry Creek to be of much use. She found a couple more lanterns and, after lighting them, took the first one out onto the porch to serve as a sign that she was there.

Someone would come looking for her sooner or later. And if they didn't come tonight, she'd simply wait until the morning and then head toward the sunrise. Payton walked over to her horse and took off his saddle, dropping it onto the front steps of the shack.

She folded the saddle blanket and threw it on top. Then she carefully tethered the horse to a hitching rail in front of the cabin before stepping inside.

The interior of the cabin was cozy and almost as comfortable as the bunkhouse, though a bit dustier. From what she could tell, the place had been used recently. There was a stack of firewood next to the cast-iron stove and canned food in the small cupboard above the dry sink. She picked through the assortment and found a can of nuts.

A shelf of paperback novels, mostly mysteries, caught Payton's attention and she chose one and sat down at the small wooden table. Though it was hard to read in the flickering light, she managed to finish a few pages before her eyes grew tired. With a frustrated sigh, she laid her head down on the table and closed her eyes.

She wasn't sure whether she'd fallen asleep or not, but a loud crash brought her upright. She saw a shadow in the doorway and screamed. But a moment later, Brody stepped into the light.

He crossed the room in a few long strides, grabbed her arms and yanked her into his embrace. "What the hell were you thinking?" he muttered. "I got back to the station and they said you'd left on horseback."

"I was just going to ride out to meet you and then my horse came up lame. I thought he'd lead me back to the stable, but he came here."

"You're on Fraser land," Brody said. He pressed a kiss to the top of her head and then took a deep breath. "Do you know how dangerous it is out here? You can walk for a day and not see anything familiar."

"That's why I decided to stay here."

"The first smart move you made all day." He cupped her face in his hands and kissed her, his mouth harsh and demanding, as if he was exacting punishment for what she'd done.

But he didn't stop there. He tore off his jacket and tossed it aside, then began to work at the buttons of her shirt. When he wasn't removing her clothes, he was stripping out of his, and within a minute, they were both naked.

Payton wasn't sure what to say. She knew he was angry and maybe a bit shaken, but he seemed to need reassurance that she was safe. He buried his face in the curve of her neck, his hands skimming over her body as if to prove to himself she was unhurt.

Brody turned her around in his arms. Payton knew what was coming, but she wasn't prepared for the intensity of his need. "I don't have protection," he murmured.

"It's all right," Payton said, arching against him. She'd taken care of birth control a long time ago, choosing a method that was both constant and convenient. She wanted to experience him without any barriers, to feel just him inside her.

He buried himself deep in a single thrust, then held her, drawing a deep breath. She wriggled against him, silently pleading for him to move, but he held her still until he regained control.

He began slowly at first, with a delicious rhythm that she couldn't deny. Her mind whirled with a maelstrom of sensation and she felt herself losing touch with reality. Every stroke brought her closer to completion.

Payton moved with him, sending him even deeper. Every movement felt like perfection, as though their bodies were made to do just this. His fingers grasped her hips as she urged him on, so close to release that she was afraid they might both collapse onto the floor before they were through.

Brody moaned and she knew he was close. But then, suddenly he stopped. "Say it," he murmured. "Tell me you'll never leave me."

At first, she wasn't sure what he meant. Did he just want to hear the words, or was he demanding the promise behind them. In the end, Payton didn't really care. If he wanted her to stay, she would, for as long as this passion lasted. "I won't," she said. "I promise."

"Promise me," he said, his voice raw as he moved again.

"I promise."

Satisfied, he brought them both closer and closer. And then, in a blinding instant, Payton cried out and dissolved into powerful spasms of pleasure. He was there with her, his body shuddering with every stroke.

Brody sighed as he kissed her nape, his teeth grazing her skin. When he stumbled, Payton steadied them both, their bodies still joined. "I think we should sit down," she said.

"No," he murmured. "I want to stay just like this."

"All right," she said, reaching back to wrap her arm around his neck. She shifted and he groaned, slipping out of her.

Brody moved over to one of the bunks and gently lowered her onto the rough wool blanket. Then he stretched out beside her. Goose bumps prickled her skin and she pulled the edges of the blanket up around them both. "It's not as comfy as your bed," she said. "But it will do."

"We're trespassing. Considering the feud between the Frasers and the Quinns, we might end up shot, or in jail."

"It was worth it," she teased.

"No more adventures in the outback for you."

"I'll just take you with me." She closed her eyes and snuggled against him. At that moment, Payton couldn't imagine ever doing without this passion. Or without this man. What that meant, she wasn't sure. But it did mean something.

"TEAGUE?"

Brody awoke to the sound of a woman's voice. The door creaked and he pushed up on his elbow, squinting against the sunlight that shone through the door, Payton still sound asleep beside him. "Brody," he said.

He heard hurried footsteps on the front steps, then carefully rolled out of bed and tugged his jeans on. When he got outside, Brody found Hayley Fraser mounting her horse.

"Wait," he called, raking his hand through his tousled hair.

She paused, watching him warily from atop her horse. Brody hadn't seen Hayley in ages, not since she and Teague were teenagers. But he had seen photos of her in magazines and on television. Teague's ex-girlfriend had become one of Australia's most popular young actresses. She had a part on a television show that almost everyone in Oz watched every Thursday evening, and there were rumors that she was about to make a move to Hollywood.

"What are you doing here?" she asked, her wavy blond hair blowing in the morning breeze.

"We needed a place to sleep. This was close by. Was Teague supposed to meet you here?"

"No," she said, an edge of defensiveness in her voice. "Why would you think that?"

"It was almost as if you were expecting him," Brody said.

"I saw the Kerry Creek horses and I thought it

might be him. But I was mistaken. Sorry. I didn't mean to wake you."

She looked even more beautiful than she did on television. But instead of being dressed in some sexy outfit, with her hair fixed up, she wore jeans, a canvas jacket and a stockman's hat. "Should I tell Teague you were looking for him?"

"Why?" She shook her head. "No. You don't need to tell him anything."

Brody felt a hand on his arm and he turned to see Payton standing beside him, wrapped in the wool blanket. "Morning," she said, nodding to Hayley.

"Payton, this is Hayley Fraser," Brody said. "Her family owns this place. Hayley, Payton Harwell."

Payton smiled. "Thank you for letting us stay here. I got lost last night and wasn't really prepared to sleep outside."

Hayley nodded, her expression cool and guarded. She'd never really warmed to anyone else in the Quinn family or anyone connected with them. In truth, Brody's parents had discouraged a relationship to the point where they forbade Teague from seeing her. At the time, both Callum and Brody had sided with their parents. But Teague had never bothered to follow their advice. And he probably wouldn't now.

"I—I have to go," Hayley murmured. "Stay as long as you like. I won't say anything to my grandfather."

She wheeled her horse around and kicked it into a gallop, the dust creating a cloud behind her. Brody and Payton watched as she rode off. Brody glanced down at Payton, then slipped his arm around her shoulders. "That was odd," he said.

"She seemed nice."

Brody laughed. "What is it with you Americans?"

"Us Americans?" Payton looked around. "There's only one American here. Are you speaking of me?"

"Yes. Why do you always have such a positive attitude about everything? Everything is always...nice. Even if it isn't, you smile and pretend it is. Why don't you just say what you think? Hayley Fraser is a bitch."

"I don't even know her. Why would I think that?" Her brow creased into a frown and she shook her head. "And why are you such a grouch?"

"See, there you go. I *am* being a grouch." He turned and walked inside, grabbing his clothes scattered across the floor. "At least you said what you thought."

"My mother always told me if I couldn't say something nice, I shouldn't say anything at all. It's hard for me to forget those little lessons."

"People aren't always perfect," he said.

"I know that. I'm not naive. But I prefer to see the positive qualities rather than dwelling on the negative."

"Like the way you look at me?" Brody asked.

Payton sat down on the edge of the bunk and began to idly pick lint off the blanket, smoothing her hand over the rough wool every now and then. "You've been very nice—I mean, you've been generous and kind and understanding. You got me out of jail, you gave me a place to live and—"

"I sleep with you. I make you moan with pleasure, I touch your body like—"

"All right. You do have a nasty sarcastic streak that comes out when you haven't had enough sleep. You're not perfect. And neither am I. So can we leave it at that?"

Was that it? Brody's jaw twitched as he tried to control his temper. He'd been so happy to find her last night he hadn't even thought about what he'd learned from the Internet. She'd run away from her family and the man she was supposed to love and for some reason, she'd decided to hide out with him.

But sooner or later, she'd get sick of life on the station, just like his mother. She'd realize she'd made a mistake and she'd be gone, back to her comfortable life with her rich husband and his fancy job. So why hadn't she told him the truth about her past?

Maybe for the same reason he hadn't told her about his past—he wasn't proud of who he'd been, or of some of the things he'd done.

"Get dressed," he said. "We need to get back. Cal will be wondering where we are."

"If there's something you want to know, all you have to do is ask," she said.

"No." He shook his head.

"I'll tell you anything."

That was the problem. Did he really want to know all the details of her relationship with a man she loved enough to marry? Did he want her making comparisons between the two of them? He ought to be happy for the time they had together and just leave it at that. Brody certainly couldn't offer her the kind of life that Sam Whitman could.

"I'm fine," he said, forcing a smile. "You're right. I'm just cranky." He walked across the room and stood in front of her.

"Don't act like such a dickhead," she muttered, sending him a sulky look.

Brody laughed, taking a step back. "Well, there you go again. I see you're learning the lingo. You could tell me not to be such a drongo."

"That, too." She drew a deep breath. "What is that?"

"A dimwit," he said. "An idiot for not appreciating you. A fool for taking my bad mood out on you." He held out his hand and when she placed her fingers in his, he gently pulled her to her feet. "So, what are we going to do with our day today?"

"I have to work in the stables. I was gone all yesterday."

"I'll help you finish."

"I bought a swimsuit, so we could hang out in the hot tub. And I bought some new underwear. I might even model it for you."

"I'm feeling my mood getting much lighter," he said. "What color?"

"Is your mood?"

"No. What color is the underwear?"

"Black," she said.

He wrapped his hands around her waist drawing her body against his. "I like black underwear."

"Every man likes black underwear."

He bent down and brushed a kiss across her lips. "You know, we could stay here a little longer. At least we have some privacy."

A tiny smile curled the corners of her mouth. "For a little while," she suggested. "But only if we go back to bed."

With a low growl, he pushed her backward until they both tumbled onto the narrow bunk. "Maybe if I have a bit more sleep I won't be so cranky."

He felt her hand on the front of his jeans. "I know exactly how to make you feel better."

"Then I'll put myself in your capable hands—or hand."

6

THE MIDDAY SUN shone in a cloudless sky. Payton stood on the fence at the edge of the paddock and watched as Callum demonstrated the fine art of campdrafting. He'd declared a holiday from all work in honor of the queen's birthday—June 8. Brody had explained that it wasn't Queen Elizabeth's real birthday, but no one seemed to care about that small technicality. A holiday was a day off, something they all needed.

The stockmen had decided a barbecue was in order and had set up an afternoon of lighthearted competition between station employees followed by a sumptuous meal. They'd begun with a brief course on one of Australia's original sports, showing Gemma and Payton how campdrafting worked.

A calf was let out of a pen into the paddock and the rider carefully herded the calf around a series of obstacles, barrels and posts. Each rider was timed and the fastest to get the calf through the obstacle course would win a cherry pie that Mary had baked for the event.

Gemma and Payton watched from behind the fence, cheering on each stockman and wildly applauding their efforts against Brody and Callum. Though Payton had only known Gemma for a week, it was easy to like her.

She was witty and audacious, yet very levelheaded, someone Payton could turn to for advice. They'd taken to meeting up midafternoon for tea with Mary, the three of them enjoying freshly baked biscuits and a cuppa, as Gemma had called it.

To the surprise of everyone, Teague had turned up halfway through the competition with Hayley Fraser in tow. At first, she'd caused quite a stir among the men. Payton had informed Gemma that, according to Brody, Hayley was a popular television star in Australia and a huge celebrity. But the extra attention seemed to only make Hayley more uncomfortable and she chose to stand alone while she watched Teague compete with his brothers.

"She looks miserable," Payton said to Gemma. "I'm going to go talk to her."

"Callum certainly hasn't done much to make her feel welcome," Gemma commented. "Men can be so thickheaded."

Payton grabbed Gemma's arm. "Come on, let's go teach those boys a little bit about hospitality."

They walked over to Hayley and stood on either side of her, their arms braced on the top bar of the fence. "You know what I love about this," Gemma chirped in her charming Irish accent. "I love the chaps. A man wearing chaps just sets my imagination to working overtime."

"Why is that?" Payton asked, playing along.

"I just can't help but think about what those things would look like without the jeans underneath." She glanced over at Payton and pulled a silly face. Payton burst out laughing and Hayley couldn't help herself. A giggle erupted from her throat and she bit her bottom lip to stop herself.

"I was thinking exactly the same thing," Hayley said. "Why do I find those things so sexy?"

"It's the leather," Gemma said. "It's so…"

"Dangerous?" Payton asked.

"Smooth," Hayley said.

"Naughty," Gemma added. "I mean, I can understand how a man would enjoy lacy underwear on a woman. For me, a man in leather just gets me all tingly."

The trio stood and silently watched as Teague maneuvered a calf through the maze of posts and barrels, the rest of the stockmen shouting directions from across the paddock.

"Thanks," Hayley said.

Payton turned to face her. "For what?"

"For making it easier. I know how Brody and Callum feel about me and I don't think they were too chuffed to see me turn up here."

"Whatever is going on in their heads has nothing to do with us," Gemma assured her.

"Sistahs before mistahs," Payton said decisively. They both looked at her as if she'd suddenly begun speaking Armenian. "Sisters before misters. Girlfriends should come before boyfriends."

"Oh," Gemma said. "Yes. I completely agree."

"Do you ride?" Gemma asked Hayley.

"Like the wind," she said with a grin. "What about you?"

"No. If they did this on bicycles I might give it a go. But horses scare the bleedin' bloomers off me. And I don't care for the way they smell either." She sighed.

"Still, I wish I knew how to ride. Callum seems to be more comfortable on a horse than on his feet."

"I could teach you," Payton said.

"Me, too," Hayley offered.

Gemma smiled. "Callum offered, but I didn't want to look like a muppet in front of him, so I begged off. But as long as I'm here, I wouldn't mind trying."

"It's a date then," Hayley said. "Payton can bring you out to the shack. I'll organize a lunch and then we can ride back together."

The idea of making plans together seemed to solidify their new friendship and as they watched the boys, they chatted amiably.

"What do you think they're talking about?" Gemma asked, nodding in the direction of the three Quinn brothers. The men sat on their horses, staring across the paddock.

"Maybe they think we're plotting against them," Payton said.

Brody was the first to approach. He smiled as he drew his horse to a stop. "Ladies," he said, tipping his hat. "Are you having a lovely time?"

Payton smiled seductively. "Absolutely," she said.

"What are you doing over here all on your own?"

"Discussing our love of chaps," Gemma said. "With or without jeans. If I might be so bold, which do you prefer?"

Her question took him by surprise and he grinned. "That's between me and my horse." He turned to Payton. "Would you ladies like to give it a go? I'm sure the boys would love to see you jump into the competition. And there are prizes to be had for the winners."

"I'll try," Payton said.

"Me, too." Hayley crawled over the fence and started in Teague's direction.

"I'm afraid I'll have to sit this one out," Gemma said.

"Come on," Brody insisted. "Callum will ride with you. You can steer and he'll work the pedals."

Gemma grinned. "All right."

Payton helped her over the fence and they strode across the paddock, Brody riding beside them. When they got to the boys, Brody suggested that they all compete in pairs to make the game more equitable. The girls would hold the reins while the boys held the girls and used the stirrups.

As the eldest, Callum went first, settling Gemma on the saddle in front of him and wrapping his arm around her waist while his other hand gripped the saddle horn. Brody and Payton watched from a spot at the fence as Davey released a calf from the pen.

He stood behind her, his chin resting on her shoulder, his hand on her hip. "So what were you girls really talking about?" he asked, his voice soft against her ear.

"Sex," she said.

"Really?"

"That's all girls talk about when they're together. We were comparing the three of you."

"And how did I fare?" he asked.

"Oh, I spoke very highly of you," Payton teased.

His hand slowly moved forward on her hip until it was pressed flat on her lower abdomen, right above the waistband of her jeans. "Did you tell them how good I am at making you moan?" His fingertips drifted a bit lower.

"Stop," Payton said. "Everyone is watching."

"No one is watching," Brody countered.

She closed her eyes and moaned softly. How was it possible that he could set her nerves on fire with a simple touch? They were both fully dressed, standing amidst a group of people, and all she could think about was his hand dipping into her pants.

"How far will you go, Payton? Can I make you come just by talking to you?"

"Don't even try," she said.

"I'll wager I can. Dare me."

"Brody, I—" He shoved his hand a bit farther beneath her waistband and she sucked in a sharp breath. "All right. You probably could. But that doesn't mean I want you to. Not here."

"Where?" he murmured.

"Your room."

"Hey!" Brody called. "We're going to grab some more coldies. Who wants one?" He took the time to count the takers then turned to Payton. "Come on, you can give me a hand."

They started off toward the house without attracting any attention. When they reached the porch, Brody pressed his finger to his lips, then poked his head inside the door. Though the smell of fresh-baked bread drifted out, Mary was elsewhere. He took Payton's hand and dragged her through the kitchen, then up the stairs, taking them two at a time.

When they were both inside his room, Brody slammed the door behind them and began to unbutton her jeans. Payton fumbled with the belt holding his chaps, but let go when he bent over to pull off her shoes. Her jeans and panties followed and by the time he stood, he was completely aroused, his erection pressing against the faded denim.

Getting him undressed was too much effort and in the end, she unbuckled his belt and pulled his jeans down around his hips. He picked her up and carried her to the bed.

In one exquisite movement, he slid inside her, her body ready for him, so wet with desire. From the moment he moved, Payton felt herself dancing near the edge. This wasn't a slow, easy seduction but a desperate attempt to possess each other.

She clutched at his shoulders, her mouth pressed against his throat. "Oh," she cried. "Oh, yes."

"Tell me you want it," he said, his voice raw with passion.

"I do," Payton said, her own desperation growing.

She felt her orgasm building, fueled by the almost violent nature of their bodies arching against each other. Every thrust became magnificent torture, pushing her closer to the edge and then drawing her back again. Payton let her mind drift, focusing on the spot where they were joined.

And then, she was there, her release shattering reality. Wave after wave of pleasure coursed through her and she felt him surrender to his own orgasm. He kept moving inside her until he couldn't move anymore. Then Brody rolled onto his back, carrying her with him.

The entire encounter had only lasted a few minutes, but Payton had never experienced anything quite so powerful. She'd wanted him so much that her desire had overwhelmed all rational thought. He owned her body and he was quickly taking possession of her soul.

"We're bad," he whispered.

"I know," Payton said. "I think it was the chaps."

Brody laughed out loud, wrapping his arm around her neck and rolling her onto her side. He faced her, his hand lazily trailing through her hair. "So all I have to do to get you into bed is wear leather?"

"I think you already know the answer to that question."

"Tell me anyway."

"You just have to touch me," Payton said softly. "That's all it takes."

He smiled boyishly, then stole another kiss. "I'll remember that." Pausing, he ran his finger along her jaw and met her gaze. "There is one thing. We haven't been using protection, and at the shack you said—"

"It's all right. There won't be any surprises."

"Good," he said. "I mean, not that surprises are always bad, but I'm not sure we're ready for that."

Sam had been obsessed about birth control, insisting that Payton find a method that would protect them both without fail. They'd been engaged and they'd always planned to have children, so Payton wondered why he'd been so adamant. Sam had acted as if an unplanned pregnancy would've been a disaster. Why hadn't she ever questioned him making such a decision about her body?

"Payton?"

She blinked, startled from her thoughts. What had brought Sam to mind? She hadn't thought of him in…days.

Brody was staring at her, a frown on his face. "What's wrong?"

Payton shook her head. "Nothing. We should probably get back outside. The boys will want their beers."

Brody levered to his feet, then held out his hand. He patiently helped her dress, patting her backside once she was completely clothed again. But as he turned for the door, Payton noticed a purple mark on his neck.

"Oh, no," she said, reaching up for his chin and tipping his head up. "Did I do that?"

"What?"

She laughed. "I think I gave you a hickey."

"What's that?" Brody asked.

She pulled him over to the mirror above his dresser and pointed to the spot on his neck.

"A love bite," he said, examining it closely. "I haven't had one of those since I was a teenager."

"Sorry."

He shrugged. "I like it. I like knowing I can make you do such things to me."

She stared at his reflection in the mirror and smiled. "I think we're both in trouble," she said.

He nodded. "I think you might be right."

"Brody!"

They both turned to see a horse approaching at a fast gallop. Davey pulled the horse to a stop, nearly running into Brody. "What the hell are you about?" Brody shouted.

"Callum," he said, gasping for breath.

"What's wrong? Is he all right?"

"Yeah. Yeah, he's fine. He needs you back at the house. Right now. He said just you, not Payton. Just you. He made that very clear."

Brody frowned. "Well, I'm not going to leave Payton out here on her own," he said.

"No, I'm to help her out," Davey said. "Go ahead. I'll carry on."

Brody regarded the young kid suspiciously. Why was it so important for Payton to stay behind? What the hell was Callum up to? He maneuvered his horse next to Payton's, then reached out and placed his hand on her cheek. "I'll be back in a bit." Brody leaned over and dropped a kiss on her lips. "Don't let Davey boss you around."

She smiled. "I won't. I'll see you later."

Brody kicked his horse into a gallop and headed toward the house. This had damn well better be an emergency. The ride back to the homestead was almost fifteen minutes. As he rode, Brody's thoughts rewound over the past few days. He and Payton had settled into a life of sorts.

She'd managed to charm Davey into working the stables for the day while she worked the station with Brody. They enjoyed the long ride together and Payton had been fascinated with discovering new plants and animals in the outback. She'd nearly fallen off her horse when she'd spotted her first kangaroo.

He liked having her with him, and Callum hadn't seemed to mind that they'd paired up. After greasing two of the windmills, they'd eaten some lunch, then set off to ride the fence lines. Payton had quickly learned how to handle herself on a stock pony, eagerly taking tips from Brody when he offered.

Still, her fascination with station life worried him. Was she happy here or was she just avoiding her real life with Sam Whitman? He needed answers, yet he couldn't bring himself to ask the question. Was she married? And if she was, did it make a difference anymore? He wasn't sure that it did for him. Not now.

Brody had been considering his options, specifically another surgery on his knee. He was still covered under the team's insurance and he really didn't have anything to lose, except a month or two off his feet and at least a year spent in rehab. He cursed softly. The more time he spent with Payton, the more confused he became about his future.

He'd always trusted his gut instinct when it came to any decision, and his gut had never steered him wrong—until the accident. The rain had made the roads slick and he'd already been late for practice, caught up in an argument with Nessa. He hadn't been paying attention and had taken a turn far too fast. As he went down, his only thought had been that he ought to have trusted his gut and taken the Land Rover to work.

Right now, every instinct told him that Payton belonged in his life, that he should to do everything in his power to keep her there. So why couldn't he just say that to her? Why couldn't he tell her how he felt? Brody had never doubted himself until now. Maybe his feelings weren't as strong as they seemed. Or maybe, this was something more than just infatuation.

As he rode past the horse paddock and into the yard, he saw Callum standing on the back porch, pacing nervously. He waited for Brody to come to a stop before jogging down the steps. Brody hopped off, gathering the reins in his hand.

"Come on," Callum murmured.

"What's up?"

"Teague is in the house. There's a private investigator here looking for Payton."

"Shit," Brody muttered. "How did he find her?"

"You know about him?"

"Yeah, he was in Bilbarra trying to track her down. I talked to him. I thought I sent him off to Sydney to look for her."

"Well, he's a little bit smarter than you reckoned," Callum said. "Payton used her credit card at David Jones in Brisbane. And Teague bought something right after her with his card. The clerk mentioned that they were together, so that's why he's here. Teague is feeding him some story, but I'm not sure if he's swallowing it."

Brody frowned. Payton had spent time in jail for dining and dashing. Why had she suddenly chosen to use a credit card? Had she wanted to be found? Was she looking for an excuse to leave? Or was she unaware that a detective had been sent to find her? "We have to get her out of here," Brody muttered.

"What the hell has she done?" Callum asked.

"I don't know." Brody cursed softly. "She was supposed to get married in April. She ran out on her wedding. And I'd assume her fiancé or her husband wants her back, since he sent someone to fetch her. Bit of a problem there since I don't want to give her back."

"Brody, she's an adult. She should make these decisions for herself. If she wants to stay, she can just tell the guy to get lost."

"And what if she doesn't?" Brody asks. "What if she decides to leave with him?"

"Then that's her choice. You can't keep her here if she doesn't want to stay."

"She may want to stay," Brody countered. "Only she isn't ready to admit it yet. She might need more time."

"Did you ever think about asking her straight out?"

"I'm not going to ask her unless I'm sure she'll give me the right answer."

"Bloody hell, Brody, just talk to the girl."

"I will," Brody promised. "Soon. But right now, I have to get her off the station. I'll go back and get her and we'll ride to the airstrip. I need you to go to the bunkhouse and gather up her things and put them in your ute. Teague can meet us out there."

"Are you sure you want to do this?" Callum asked.

The backdoor squeaked and Teague stepped outside. The moment he saw Brody, he grabbed him by the arm and pulled him around the side of the house. "What the hell is going—"

"Don't ask," Brody said. "I'll explain it all later. Can you get away or is this guy going to follow you wherever you go?"

"I think I can lose him. Why?"

"I need you to fly Payton and me to Brisbane. I'm going to go and get her and we'll meet you at the airstrip. Callum is going to put her things in his ute. Whenever you can, get away and meet us there."

"All right," Teague said, nodding. "I better get back in there. He thinks I'm making coffee."

Brody jumped on his horse and turned it away from the house. "We'll be at the airstrip in a half hour," he said. "Don't let him follow you."

The ride in had taken twice as long as the ride back. He rode as hard and as fast as he'd ever ridden, as if his life depended upon it. In the end, his life did depend upon Payton. He'd grown attached to her and he couldn't imagine losing her, especially to another man.

He found them where he'd left them, working on a broken gate that led to the east horse pasture. Davey was holding the gate off the ground while Payton twisted the turnbuckle. They both stopped what they were doing and watched as he approached.

"Get on your horse," he told Payton. "Come on, we have to go."

"What's wrong?" she asked.

"I'll tell you after we get to the airstrip."

"Why are we going to the airstrip?"

"Payton, don't ask any questions. Just get on your horse and let's ride."

She studied him for a long moment, then handed Davey the spanner she was holding. Snagging her jacket from where she'd thrown it over the gate, she kept her gaze fixed on him. Then, in an easy motion, she put her foot in the stirrup and swung her leg over the saddle.

Brody didn't take the time to explain any further. He simply wheeled his mount around and took off, hoping she'd follow. A few seconds later, she caught up to him and they rode through the scrub, a cloud of dust forming behind them.

Their horses were winded by the time they reached the airstrip. Brody dismounted and then helped Payton do the same. He slapped both horses on the rump and sent them running, knowing they'd find their way back to the stables on their own.

"Are you going to explain what we're doing here?" Payton asked.

"First, you have to tell me something. And I want you to be completely honest, because I'll be able to tell if you're lying to me."

"All right," she said softly.

Brody grabbed her by the arms and pulled her toward him, his mouth coming down on hers. He softened the kiss immediately, hoping that it would serve as a last attempt to prove his feelings for her. Then he drew back and took a deep breath. "Are you married? Did you go through with your wedding or did you walk out before you said 'I do'?"

Her mouth dropped open and she stared at him in utter shock. "How do you know about—"

"Just answer the question. Are you married?"

"I…" She paused, as if she wasn't sure how to answer him. "No. Of course not. If I were married, I'd be with my husband. I certainly wouldn't be sleeping with you. How did you know about my wedding?"

"We have the Internet here, too."

She took a moment, then shook her head. "You Googled me?"

"Yes. And a private investigator tracked you here," he replied. "You used your credit card in Brisbane and he figured out where you were."

She groaned, closing her eyes and shaking her head. "I knew I shouldn't have used the card. I didn't use it earlier for food. But I thought since I was flying right back to the station, it wouldn't make a difference. They wouldn't be able to find me even if they were watching the card."

"Turns out Teague bought something at the same time and he used his card. They figured out you two were together." He rubbed her forearms. "I think you should tell me what's going on, Payton. Tell me about Sam Whitman."

She sucked in a sharp breath and looked at him, her eyes wide. "You know about— But, how—"

"It doesn't matter. Just tell me what happened."

She drew a deep breath. "I ran out on the wedding before we got to the vows." She took his hand. "I should have told you. But I wanted to leave that part of my life behind."

"Why did you run?"

She shrugged. "I'm not sure. I just had this feeling that I was making a huge mistake. I honestly can't say what it was. I'm not an impetuous person, but I had this—" She put her hand on her stomach.

"Gut feeling?"

"Yes," she said, as if his explanation suddenly made perfect sense of her actions.

"So what does your gut tell you to do now?" Brody asked. "We can ride back to the house and you can talk to this guy. Or we can leave. Teague will fly us to Brisbane and from there we'll catch a flight to Perth."

"Perth?"

"I have an apartment in Fremantle, just across the river. We can hang out until the investigator leaves."

She considered the offer for a long moment. "And then what?" she asked. "I can't avoid my family forever."

"Then we'll go back to the station right now and you can call them."

He waited as she weighed her options, hoping and praying that she'd choose to leave with him. He knew he'd have to let her go sooner or later, but he wasn't ready. He'd take another day, another week, as much time as he could get.

"I don't know what I want," she said.

He'd asked her if she was married and he'd gotten the right answer. But the second question had gone unasked. Was she still in love with her fiancé? The words were on the tip of his tongue, but he was afraid of what she might say. Right now, he'd rather not know.

He reached up and cupped her face in his hands. "Come with me to Fremantle," he said. Leaning forward, he kissed her again, softly, a silent plea.

"All right," she said. "For a little while. We'll go to Fremantle."

Brody released a tightly held breath and yanked her into his arms. He had a few more days, a week even. And this time, he wasn't going to waste it. He'd savor every second he spent with her. They'd walk on the beach and make love all night and sleep until noon and then do it all over again the next day. And, maybe, she'd decide she never wanted to leave at all.

BY THE TIME they landed at the airport in Perth, Payton had filled in the details of her story, from her parents' high expectations, to her belief that Sam was the man she was supposed to marry. And then she told him about her sudden decision to break free from the path that had been laid out for her. Until that moment, she'd simply deferred to her parents and her fiancé.

It felt good to pick apart her life, to examine her motives and try to make sense of them. And it almost gave her enough courage to call her parents and apologize for everything that she'd put them through. But after a half day's work on the station and two separate plane trips, she was exhausted. The thought of making that phone call twisted her stomach into knots.

"I know what you're thinking." She sighed, avoiding his gaze as they walked from the plane.

He held her hand, his fingers laced through hers. "No, you don't," Brody said.

"You think I'm…naive. Spineless. And maybe I am—or was. But I'm not that way anymore."

He pulled her to a stop, forcing her to face him. "Are you under the impression that this has changed the way I feel about you?" Brody asked.

"It hasn't?"

He shook his head. "No. Not at all."

They took a cab from the airport to Brody's apartment. Payton was curious about what she'd find on the other side of the front door. The building was luxurious, with its richly appointed lobby and thickly carpeted hallways. Brody hadn't told her much about his life off the station. What she knew had come from Teague—a career in football, the accident that had ruined his knee and a retreat back to the station.

He reached for the front door, then paused. "I don't remember what it looks like inside," he said, forcing a smile. "It's been a while since I've been home and I had to let my cleaning lady go." He shoved the key into the lock. "Maybe I should just check it out."

"It's all right," Payton said. "I've been working in a stable. Unless you have a dozen horses in there, nothing is going to freak me out."

Brody chuckled. "All right." The door swung open

and he stepped aside to let her enter first. She walked inside slowly, taking in the details of the interior.

It was a beautiful apartment, sleek and modern. A wall of windows overlooked the water and filled the apartment with light. It was furnished sparsely yet fashionably.

Payton wandered over to the windows and took in the view of a wide river and the city on the other side. "It's wonderful," she said. "So different from the station."

"One of the guys on the team gave me the name of his decorator. I didn't pick this stuff out myself. I would have been content with a couch and telly and a bed."

She stared up at a painting hanging on the wall above the sofa. "Very nice. So, is this what football buys?"

Brody smiled. "That's what football bought. Footy doesn't buy anything anymore."

"It's difficult to imagine you doing that. Dressed in all that gear."

"Aussie rules is not like American football," he said. "We don't wear anything but a shirt, shorts and shoes. It's more like rugby than what you think of as football." He paused. "So you know how I found out about your wedding. How did you find out about my busted career?"

"Your brother Teague. He said you were good, but that your motorcycle accident ended your career."

Brody nodded. "I was. I was the top scorer on our team. But that doesn't really matter anymore. Now some other bloke is the top scorer on the team. And I'm just a guy who spends his time working a cattle station in Queensland."

"There's nothing wrong with that," she said.

"It's not the same as being famous."

Payton ran her hands through her hair. "I'm still dirty from work. Can I take a shower?"

Brody took her bag off his shoulder. "The bathroom is through the bedroom," he said, pointing to a door in the far wall. "I'll show you."

She followed him into the bedroom and he set her bag on the bed, then turned and helped her out of her jacket. He smoothed his hands over her shoulders and nuzzled his nose in her hair. "It's nice to have you here," he said. "All to myself."

Payton leaned back against his chest and drew his arms around her. "It is funny how things work out. We've both lived such different lives, and then they touched for a moment in that jail cell. If you hadn't drunk so much beer or I'd paid for my meal, we would never have met. Gemma thinks it was fate."

"Maybe it was."

Payton turned in his arms and then pushed up on her toes and kissed him. She slipped her arms around his neck and drew him more deeply into the kiss, loving the way he tasted, the way his mouth fit so perfectly with hers. Just a simple kiss was all it took to ignite her desire.

She reached up and tugged his jacket down over his arms, then moved to work on the buttons of his shirt. They'd undressed each other so many times that it had become second nature to them. There was no longer any hesitation or embarrassment. They felt more comfortable out of their clothes than in them.

When they were both naked, he took her hand and led her into the bathroom. The shower was surrounded by glass block from floor to ceiling. He opened a door and stepped inside, turning the water on and then helping her inside when it was the proper temperature.

It was a shower made for a man who came home with bruises and sore muscles: a variety of shower-heads angled in all different directions. The door kept the steam inside and before long, the moisture created a fog around them both.

His hands smoothed over her body and she closed her eyes and enjoyed his caress. He turned her around and pulled her against him, his growing erection pressing against her backside. His palms slowly ran the length of her torso, from her breasts to her belly and then to the juncture of her thighs.

He delved between the soft folds of her sex and when he found the spot, began to touch her in a way he knew so well. Payton arched back, wrapping her arm around his neck and pulling him into another kiss.

But he wasn't content to just touch her. His mouth moved over her shoulder, his tongue tracing a path to the curve of her neck. Brody gently urged her to sit on the low bench at the center of the shower. And then he knelt in front of her, spreading her legs and continuing the seduction with his tongue.

Payton had always felt this was the most intimate ex-pression of desire and until now, they'd both been sat-isfied with other things. But Payton let go of the last shred of inhibition, surrendering to Brody, the shudders rocking her body. And as she surrendered to him, she realized that this was no longer just physical. She'd grown to need him in so many other ways.

She felt tears press at the corners of her eyes, but when he met her gaze she forced a smile. How could she ever consider living without him? He'd become part of her life, the new life that she'd found in Australia.

But was she really ready to walk away from her past, from her family and everything she'd known, to stay here with him? Payton reached up and brushed his wet hair from his eyes. She didn't need to tell him how she felt. It was understood between them, communicated by smiles and sighs and soft kisses in the dark.

Brody drew her slowly to her feet and then led her out of the shower. Her release only made her exhaustion more acute and when he wrapped her in a thick cotton towel, Payton closed her eyes and leaned against him for support.

They ended up on the bed, Brody stretched out beside her, his fingers gently stroking her cheek. "Tell me about him," he said softly. "Why did you love him?"

"That's a question," she said. "I'm not sure I have an answer."

"Try," he said. "Please?"

"I thought he was right for me. And I knew my parents would love him. I always tried to do what I thought they wanted me to. I was a very good girl."

"But there must have been something about this guy," Brody said.

"We were together so long, I guess I forgot what it was that attracted me in the first place. He was supposed to be perfect for me."

Brody was silent for a long moment, then drew a deep breath. "Do you still love him?"

"I'm not sure I ever did," Payton said. "At least not the way a woman should love the man she marries."

He seemed to take comfort in that answer. But did it make a difference? She was here, with him, running away from all her problems. She hadn't thought about how this might end between them. It was so simple to believe they would just continue, without any difficulties. They were living off the high of their infatuation. Real life hadn't intruded yet. But it would soon enough.

7

"PADDLE, PADDLE, PADDLE!" Brody shouted. He gave the surfboard a final shove, sending Payton off into the set of small waves on Cottesloe Beach. They'd practiced on the beach first and then he'd caught a few waves with her in front of him on his board. But she was determined to do it on her own.

"Pop up!" he called.

To Brody's surprise, she nimbly got to her feet. Steadying herself, she slowly straightened, her arms out to the side. Brody shouted as she rode the wave. There wasn't much that Payton couldn't do once she set her mind to something.

She stayed on her feet all the way to the shore, hopping off the board just before she hit the beach. She looked at him, waving and jumping up and down in excitement. Then she turned the board around and paddled back out to him.

The weather was perfect for a winter day in June. The sun was shining but the water was a bit chilly, so they both wore wet suits. Brody had made a gift of the surfboard and wet suit, hoping that they'd be staying in Fremantle long enough to enjoy them.

Life was certainly simpler here than it had been at

the station. Their days and nights belonged entirely to them. They strolled the streets, stopping to eat or browse through a shop when they wanted. They went to the movies and a concert in the park and rented bicycles to tour old Fremantle.

Brody had planned a trip to Rottnest Island for the next week, booking a room in the old hotel in case they wanted to spend a few hours alone together during the day. Though he knew she might decide to leave at any time, he wanted to believe she'd still be with him in a week.

They kept themselves busy during the day, but it was the nights that Brody found most satisfying. Blessed with absolute privacy, they had the time to explore the limits of their passion. Sex ranged from a silly romp, to a frantic drive for release, to a slow, methodical seduction—and all in one day.

"Did you see me?"

"I did," Brody said as she paddled up to him. "You were great."

"I was! It was so much fun. I want to try a bigger wave."

"All right, hang on. I'll just put in your order." He looked up at the sky. "Can we have some bigger waves, please?"

She splashed water in his face. "I meant, we should go to another beach with bigger waves."

He splashed her back, then reached out and grabbed her, both of them tumbling off their surfboards. Treading water, Brody pulled her into his arms and kissed her, his mouth searching for hers through the saltwater that dripped from her hair.

There was nothing more satisfying, he mused as he teased at her tongue. The fact that he could kiss and touch her whenever he chose to was something he had come to appreciate. In truth, he couldn't imagine doing without it.

He drew back and looked down into her eyes. Droplets of water clung to her lashes. "We'll find some bigger waves tomorrow," he said. He helped her back onto her board, then straddled his. "We need to get you in to shore and put some sunscreen on your face. You're starting to burn."

"Let me try one more wave. Then we can go."

"Only if you kiss me again," he said.

She leaned into him, her feet dangling off the sides of her board, and placed a quick kiss on his lips.

He frowned. "You can do better."

With a dramatic sigh, she leaned in again and this time, treated him to a full-on tongue kiss, her mouth warm against his. She knew exactly how he liked to be kissed and she used that knowledge to her advantage. When she drew back, she arched her eyebrow.

"All right," he agreed. "One more wave. I'm not going to give you a push this time. I'm just going to tell you when to go."

She lined her board up, watching over her shoulder as the next set rolled in. "Tell me when," she said.

"Go," he said. "Paddle hard. Paddle!"

This time, she got up right away. But she was so excited that she threw her arms over her head and disrupted her balance. She wobbled and then tumbled off the board into the water. Brody waited for her to come up and when she didn't, he paddled over to her board, cutting through the water in strong, even strokes.

By the time he reached her, she was up and

coughing water, clinging to the edge of the board. "Are you all right?"

She nodded. "Water up my nose." She coughed again. "That was bad."

"You shouldn't have put your hands up," he said. "You were doing so well." He held her board as she climbed back on. When they reached the shore, he helped her tuck her board under her arm before walking onto the beach.

"It's getting late," he said. "We should get some lunch." He jammed the surfboards into the sand, then peeled his wet suit down around his waist.

Payton took a deep breath and turned her face up to the sun. "I love it here. It's just like California. Only no earthquakes."

"I wish it was spring," he said. "We could go bush-walking and see the wildflowers. Western Australia is known for that. Miles and miles of flowers."

"Maybe we can," she said.

Brody knew it was just an offhand reply, that her words contained no promises. They hadn't made any plans or given any pledges to each other, beyond the promise of unbridled passion in the bedroom. He didn't want to think about that now. Instead, he was determined to show her exactly how much fun life was with him here in Oz.

"What do you want to do with the rest of the day?"

"I want to enjoy the good weather." She glanced over at him. "I noticed there's a football game this weekend. Could we go?"

"Why would you want to do that?"

"I'm just curious to see what you used to do for a living."

"I don't know," he said, shaking his head. "I haven't been to a game since I got dropped from the club."

"It's all right," she said. "If you don't want to, we don't have to."

He thought about her request for a few seconds. Denying her anything was impossible. And what did he have to lose? It might be fun to explain the game to her. There was nothing quite like Aussie football. "All right. I'm going to call and see if I can get us some decent seats."

She grinned. "Good."

"Any other requests?"

"I heard there was a nude beach around here."

"Yes," he said. "Swanbourne Beach."

"I've never been to a nude beach. I think I should try it at least once. I was really good at skinny-dipping, so I think I'd do well at the nude beach."

"You do realize you'd have to take off your clothes and go naked in front of strangers, don't you?"

"Yes. That's the point. I've never done that. I'm trying new things. Trusting my instincts. And it might feel good, liberating, don't you think?" She reached out and ran a finger down his chest. "It'll be fun."

"No," Brody said emphatically. "I'm not taking you to Swanbourne. You can go on your own if you like, but I'm not going."

"Prude," she teased. "You have a very nice body. And you're well endowed. There's nothing to be ashamed of."

"That's not it. You know exactly what happens to me when you get naked. And I'm not going to walk around the beach with a throb in my knob."

"I'd find that visual very entertaining," she said. She glanced down and fixed her gaze on his crotch.

"Stop," he said.

"What? I'm not doing anything."

"Stop it. You're going to get me all worked up."

"I'm not doing anything," she repeated in a voice filled with mock innocence.

"There's no extra room in this wet suit," he said. "So just knock it off."

She looked up at him and gave him a devilish smile. "I have such amazing powers," she said. "I surprise even myself."

He pulled her against him, wrapping his arm around her neck in a playful headlock. "Why don't we go home and you can give me a demonstration of your powers."

"I'd be happy to," she said. "I think it's important that I share my powers with as many people as I can."

"Now you've gone too far," he said, kissing the top of her head. "There will be no sharing."

They gathered their things and walked back to the car, Payton's hand tucked in his. It had been another perfect day, he mused as they strapped their boards on the BMW's roof rack. Brody couldn't imagine life getting any better than this.

PAYTON CLUTCHED the program in her hands as they walked through the crowds of fans to their seats. Brody's appearance seemed to cause quite a stir among those in attendance and he was stopped again and again with requests for autographs and photos. Payton waited patiently, watching as he handled each request with surprising grace and enthusiasm, giving special attention to the younger fans.

She hadn't realized how famous he was and she

found herself regretting her request to come. It couldn't be easy to answer all the questions about his injury, about the chances of him playing again, about the plays that everyone remembered him making.

When he finally pulled himself away from the fans, she held on to his arm and gave it a squeeze. "I'm sorry," she said.

"For what?"

"For asking you to come here. I didn't realize how difficult it might be for you. It was selfish of me."

"No," he said. "Actually, I'm doing all right. I thought it would be a bit dodgy, but it's not that bad."

They found their seats and settled in. Payton took a good look around, then turned to him. "All right, give me the scoop."

"You want ice cream?" he asked.

"No, the scoop. The skinny. The 4-1-1. Tell me what I need to know."

"Oh, all right. Well, this is the Subiaco Oval. And that's the team, my former team, out there warming up."

"The field is round," Payton said.

"Oval."

"I like the outfits," she added, observing the players on the field. "Not as hot as chaps, but pretty sexy. Nice short shorts. And sleeveless jerseys to show off the muscles." In truth, she could imagine Brody running around in that uniform. "Maybe you could take out your old outfit when we get home and we could play footballer and the surfer girl."

Brody laughed, glancing around to see if anyone had heard. "Better yet, I'll buy you a guernsey, you wear it and nothing else, and I'll show you some of my moves."

"A guernsey. Is that like a jumper or a cardie?"

"Jumper," he said. "Cardie has buttons down the front."

"And what is the team called?" she asked.

"Their official name is the Fremantle Football Club, but everyone calls them the Dockers. See, they have an anchor on their jumpers."

She nodded. "So, what's the deal? How do they get points?"

She listened as he explained the rules. Eighteen players on a side. The aim was to kick the ball through the poles on each end of the field. They could throw, kick and pass the ball to move it downfield, but they weren't supposed to hold on to it. When they kicked the ball through the center pair of four posts the team scored six points. But Payton became hopelessly confused when Brody tried to explain something called a "behind."

The game began and the crowd immediately grew noisy. She'd never been to an American football game, but she couldn't imagine more of a party atmosphere than she was experiencing now. There was music and cheering and dancing in the stands, along with a lot of beer. And incredibly dangerous activity on the field.

The players wore no padding or helmets, yet they seemed to slam into each other on a regular basis. Men were thrown to the ground and bloodied by flying elbows and knees. Payton was grateful that Brody was sitting safely next to her. She couldn't imagine watching him and not worrying herself sick.

Brody cheered the team, shouting out his displeasure at good plays by the opposition. As the game went on, he continued to explain the intricacies of the plays and by the time it ended, Payton actually could follow each play as it developed on the field.

The Dockers lost, but Brody didn't appear to be too upset by the result. In truth, he seemed to be quite happy that they'd come. Payton wrapped her arm around his waist as they walked out of the stadium.

"Brody Quinn!"

They stopped and Brody turned, then smiled as an older gentleman approached them dressed in a polo shirt with the Fremantle team logo stitched on the chest.

"Simon. How are you?"

"I'm well. You look grand. Healthy. Keeping fit, I see."

"Trying," Brody said, rubbing his abdomen. He turned to Payton. "Simon, this is Payton Harwell. Payton, this is the team doctor, Simon Purvis. He helped me through my rehab."

Simon held out his hand and Payton took it. "Pleasure," he said. "Did you enjoy the game?"

"I did," Payton said. "It's a little rougher than I expected, but it was fun to watch."

"We're a tough lot here in Oz." Simon grinned. "So, you're from America. I recognize the accent."

"I am," Payton said.

"Where do you call home?"

"Connecticut. Though I live in Manhattan. New York City?"

"Ah. New York Giants. New York Jets. Interesting. Almost bizarre, that."

"What?" Brody asked.

"I just met a scout for the Americans. For their NFL. He's come looking for kickers. I wasn't about to send any of our guys to see him. But you might want to give him a tingle, Brody."

"No," Brody said. "I'm in no condition to play."

"There's the thing," Simon said. "It's a different game. At least for kickers and punters. All you have to do is kick. They put the ball down and you kick it through the posts. Or you drop-kick it. They call that punting. Once or twice, they might knock you down, but if they touch you while you're kicking, it's a penalty. Brody, you've got a way with that foot of yours. It would be a shame to see it go to waste."

Payton turned to Brody, trying to read his expression. But she could see nothing that indicated how he felt. She expected him to be happy, or at least curious about the possibility. "I don't know. I was going to look into that surgery you told me about, but I'm not sure I—"

"You might not need the surgery," Simon said. "You don't have to carry the ball. There's no cutting or quick direction shifts. You might have to tackle, but that's really not your job." He paused. "I can ring him up, if you like. I'm sure he'd be interested in seeing you."

"I'll think about it," Brody said.

"Don't think too long," Simon warned. "He's only going to be here for a few weeks and then he's back to the States."

Brody shook Simon's hand, and as they walked back to the car, he was strangely silent. Payton wasn't sure whether he wanted her opinion on the matter, and decided to wait for him to speak first. But when he didn't, she decided to start the conversation. "That was interesting," she said. "But what is a tingle? And why do you have to give this guy one?"

"A phone call," he explained. "You know, there have been a couple of Aussies that have gone over to play in America. One was a kicker. He did pretty well."

"Do you want to play again?"

"Sure. But Aussie football is what I do."

"Have you ever seen an American game?"

"The Super Bowl once or twice. I never really paid much attention." He shook his head. "It's a crazy idea. They're not going to want anything to do with me once they see my knee."

"Maybe you could wear long pants. And show them how you can kick first, before you tell them about your injury."

Brody chuckled. "That might work. But the first thing they're going to ask is whether I've been seriously injured."

"It wouldn't hurt to talk to the guy," Payton said.

Brody opened the door of the car for her and helped her inside. "I'll think about it."

As they made their way out of the parking lot, Brody was lost in his thoughts. He held her hand, his fingers woven through hers, and every now and then, he brought her hand up to his lips and kissed it, as if to remind himself she was still there.

Payton drew a deep breath and then relaxed back into the seat. She wasn't quite sure how she felt about the possibility of him moving to the States. Here in Australia, she was the visitor. If things didn't work out, she could always leave. But having Brody in the U.S. seemed like such a serious shift in their relationship.

It was silly to worry over it now, though. When she

had to make a choice, she'd make a choice. And until then, she intended to enjoy her time with Brody.

BRODY STARED at the ceiling above the bed in the early-morning light. Sleep hadn't come easily for him, though he and Payton had exhausted themselves making love before she'd curled up in his arms and drifted off.

Instead, his head was filled with thoughts about the day's revelations. His life had taken so many sharp turns lately, he shouldn't be surprised at this one. Playing in America would give him a chance to get his life set up again. He'd be working, making a decent salary. He could save his money, instead of blowing it on expensive toys and exotic vacations. He'd have something to offer Payton then. But the chances of getting a job in the U.S. were slim, especially considering his injury.

Brody rolled over onto his side and stared at her. Her hand was curled next to her face, her hair tumbled over her shoulder. He still thought she was the most beautiful woman he'd ever met. There were moments when he believed he'd never be able to do without her, that waking up with her by his side and falling asleep with her in his arms was the only thing that mattered.

He reached out and smoothed his hand over her hip, her skin like silk beneath his fingertips. How was it that she suited him so perfectly? Whether they were living on the station or here in Fremantle, their lives seemed to mesh flawlessly.

He'd had his share of high-maintenance women—girls like Vanessa, who'd demanded far too much and offered far too little. They'd been extras in his life, like fast cars and expensive electronics, something to acquire and then grow bored with over time.

But he'd never felt as if he'd acquired Payton. She'd appeared in his life one day and decided to stay. He was well aware that she might choose to leave at any time. He wasn't in control of this relationship, she was. And maybe that's what kept the boredom at bay.

He was almost afraid to believe they might make it work. He'd always assumed he'd find the right woman, but he'd imagined it would happen at a distant point in the future, not now. She was the right woman. Brody was fairly certain of that.

So what was required to keep her? He needed a way to support them both, to give her a comfortable lifestyle. Without a job, he could give her four or five years. With a job, maybe a lifetime. And he needed to make sure her fiancé was out of her life for good. He ought to encourage her to contact her parents and smooth out the problems there. And then he needed to plead his case to her family.

Hell, they'd probably be suspicious of him from the start. He didn't come from some blueblood line with money coming out of his arse. He was a working-class bloke without a proper education. But he had one thing going for him—there wasn't another man in the world who loved Payton more than he did.

He drew a deep breath. He loved her. It was that simple. Brody gasped, stunned by the revelation. *Love* was the only way to describe how he felt.

But how did she feel? Payton had been silent on that issue. She seemed content to just go along as they were—lovers, friends, companions. She lived in the present, avoiding any discussion of what was to come.

Why was that? Brody wondered. Was it because she thought their relationship had no future? Or was it because she didn't want to face returning to her fiancé and family? If she truly loved him, she would have given him some hint by now. Every other woman he'd known was ready to profess love after the second date.

Maybe he just didn't measure up. Maybe she was biding her time until some other man caught her eye. Brody rolled over on his back and pressed his palm to his chest, aware of the ache in his heart. He'd never loved a woman before, so he'd never risked getting hurt. For the first time in his life, he was afraid. What if she didn't want him? Would he ever be able to forget her and move on?

He sat up and swung his legs over the edge of the bed, and pushed himself to his feet. Raking his hands through his hair, he wandered over to the windows and stared out at the river and the lights twinkling from the opposite side.

If he was going to make this work, he needed a plan. Hell, Callum was the planner in the family. Maybe he ought to go to his older brother for advice. Worst-case scenario, he could always work the station. They'd have a home and Payton seemed to enjoy living there. Best case, he'd find a job that allowed them to live wherever they wanted, on the station, in Fremantle, in Manhattan, if they chose.

Sighing softly, Brody walked out of the bedroom and into the kitchen. He grabbed a jug of orange juice and unscrewed the top, then took a long drink. Suddenly, he was wide awake, his mind spinning with the possibilities. If he couldn't play, maybe he could coach. Or he could be an analyst for one of the networks. Or a sports presenter on the local news.

Brody strode into the living room and picked up the remote, then flipped through the stations until he came to ESPN Australia. The network played mostly American sports, but there was a nightly program that focused on Aussie sports. He could talk football and rugby and make a paycheck doing it. And if ESPN didn't want him, perhaps he might convince someone to hire him at Seven Network.

He leaned back into the sofa and closed his eyes. His coaches and friends had all told him he could find a career outside football, but he'd been too stubborn to listen to them, too angry about his injury to even consider the alternatives. But now he had a reason to get serious about his future.

He switched the telly over to a DVD of his rookie season, listening to the analysts as they described the action. His attention shifted to the twenty-year-old kid in the green guernsey. It was hard to believe he'd ever been that young. Though it was only six years ago, it seemed like a lifetime.

"What are you doing out here?"

He turned to see Payton standing in the bedroom doorway. She'd pulled on the Dockers jumper he'd bought her at the game and she looked irresistible in it, her hair a riot of curls around her face.

"Just watching some telly," he said. He patted the sofa cushion next to him and she crossed the room and curled up beside him.

"Is this your team?" she asked.

"Yep. See, there I am. Number fifteen. Watch. I'll

score a goal." He waited, knowing every play by heart. This was the game when he'd broken the season scoring record for rookies. "There. There it is."

"Yay for you," Payton said, patting his belly. "Good onya."

He wrapped his arm around her neck and pulled her closer, pressing a kiss into her fragrant hair. "I want you to stay with me," he murmured.

"I'm not sleepy," she said, mistaking his request.

"No, I mean, I want you to stay with me. I want you to live with me, here, in Australia. I don't want you to go back to the States." He'd made the same request back at the shack that night she got lost in the bush. But then, he'd just wanted reassurance. Now, he wanted to focus on the future.

She pushed back and looked up into his eyes, her brow creased in an intense frown. "I'm not going anywhere."

"Promise me," he said. "I don't want to wake up some morning and find you gone. I want to make this work."

She sighed softly, then glanced away. "I'm here because I want to be, Brody. If I didn't want to be here, I'd tell you."

"Would you? You ran out on your wedding. You didn't tell your fiancé that you didn't want to be there."

"That was different," Payton said.

"How? Tell me how."

"I—I…" She paused for a moment, then shook her head. "I should have been brave enough to tell him the truth. I don't have any excuses for that. But I'm different now. I'm not afraid to speak up for myself, for what I want. I promise, I'll tell you if I want to leave."

It wasn't the promise he was looking for, but it was as good as he was going to get. Brody would have to be satisfied that it was enough. And yet he wasn't. Until Payton faced her family and her ex-fiancé, he'd always be looking over his shoulder, waiting for someone to turn up and lure her back to the States.

Did he really want to live with that kind of doubt? A sensible, secure guy would tell her to go back and clear up the mess she'd made and then return to him, free of any entanglements. But Brody had never cared for any woman the way he cared for Payton. And he didn't want to let her out of his sight for a moment, much less send her toddling back to Mr. Moneybags.

"Do you ever think about him?" Brody asked.

"Sam?"

Sam. There. She'd said his name. How many times had she said that name? How many times with love in her eyes and how many times with passion in her touch? She had a whole history with this man, a life that Brody knew nothing about.

"Never mind." He pushed to his feet. "I don't need to know. I really don't want to know." He raked his hands through his hair again, suddenly feeling a bit vulnerable, standing in front of her stark naked. This was exactly why he couldn't allow himself to believe in a future with Payton.

She might be able to handle it, but he'd surely find a way to fuck it up. "I'm going to go for a run," he said.

"But, it isn't even light out."

Brody shrugged. "It will be by the time I get back."

"I could come with you."

"No. I just need to clear my head." He walked back

to the bedroom and put on a pair of shorts and a T-shirt, then grabbed his trainers from the closet floor. When he returned to the living room, she was sitting where he'd left her, her knees pulled up beneath the oversize jumper.

"I'll be back in an hour," he said. "Why don't you get a little more sleep and then we'll go to breakfast."

Brody slipped out of the door before she could reply to his suggestion, then strode down the hall to the lift. He stepped inside, releasing a tightly held breath as the doors closed in front of him.

There was no sense trying to plan his future right now. Until he found work, it would be best to keep his feelings for Payton in check. He could enjoy their time together, enjoy the passion they shared, but anything beyond that would be a risk.

8

PAYTON STROLLED slowly through the Fremantle Market, searching for inspiration for the evening meal. She'd already purchased prawns at the fish market on the harbor and now she was studying the vegetables that filled the stalls.

Though they'd only been in Fremantle for a week and a half, she'd already settled into life with Brody. They'd spent their days touring the city and surfing and trying new restaurants. Yesterday, they'd sailed a friend's boat to Rottnest Island and ridden bicycles over the picturesque roads. Brody had even rented a room at the old hotel where they had their lunch and enjoyed a "nap" before continuing their tour.

Payton smiled to herself. Though they'd stripped off their clothes before crawling into bed, neither one of them had had any intention of sleeping. Instead, they'd spent a lazy hour kissing and touching before they made love.

It had been a wonderful day filled with long walks and quiet conversation. Brody was a complicated man, troubled by his own doubts and worries. He'd confessed that he was toying with the idea of calling the NFL scout and talking to him about a job.

Though she could sense his tension over scheduling

a tryout, Payton tried to reassure him that even if it didn't work out, it didn't represent a failure. In the end, Brody made the call.

The NFL scout had arranged to meet him at the Oval tomorrow. Brody had nearly canceled, but she'd convinced him she would be there when he came home, exactly as she was when he left, whether the tryout was a success or not.

The more she got to know Brody, the more she realized how vulnerable he was when it came to his emotions. He seemed so self-assured on the outside, but inside, he was a tangle of insecurities. There were moments when she caught him watching her, times when she woke up and he was clutching her hand so tightly it hurt. Was he really that afraid of losing her?

Though Payton had left a mess in Fiji, she didn't have any plans to return home. She would have to call at some point and had resolved to do that by the end of the week. The private investigator was probably still searching for her and it wouldn't do to waste more of her parents' money or cause them any more worry.

By now, they should be comfortable with the fact that she wouldn't be coming home anytime soon. They'd have accepted the notion that Sam would not be her husband and that she would not be living a comfortable life in Connecticut, raising their grandchildren and attending charity events.

She shook her head, a tiny shudder running through her at the thought. How close to that life had she come? If she'd pushed aside her fears and married Sam, it would have been her future—everything all planned out in front of her.

But her life with Brody was exciting. Every day was a new adventure. And though he worried about his career, Payton was truly convinced that she could live anywhere with him and be happy. She loved working at the station. And she loved Fremantle, too. But most of her affection for both places had come from being with Brody.

Payton strolled over to a vegetable stall and chose some colorful sweet peppers and fingerling potatoes. She waited for the vendor to put them in a bag for her. Then she moved on to the nearest fruit stall and picked out some red oranges, knowing they would make a wonderful tangy-sweet sauce for the prawns. At the last second, she picked up a kilo of strawberries for dessert.

It wasn't a long walk back to Brody's apartment and the weather was pleasant. She'd bought only enough for the evening meal and didn't mind carrying the bags.

As she approached Brody's building, she noticed a dark sedan parked across the street. A man was standing against the front fender, his arms crossed over his chest. He saw her almost immediately and Payton's breath caught as he removed his glasses.

"Sam," she whispered to herself. Her heart slammed against her rib cage as he slowly crossed the street to where she stood. She blinked, hoping that she was seeing things, but as he came closer, Payton knew he wasn't a figment of her imagination.

"Hello, Payton," he said. He reached out and grabbed her elbow, then brushed a kiss on her cheek.

"Hello, Sam. What are you doing here?"

He gave her a cool look, his icy blue eyes cutting through her. "What do you think, Payton?"

She opened her mouth, then snapped it shut. She didn't know what to say.

"Don't worry," he muttered. "I'll wait for your answer. I'm used to that."

His words dripped with sarcasm. She hadn't realized until now, but that was one of things she truly hated about Sam. When he was angry, he got nasty. She'd always just accepted it as part of his nature, but now she realized there were men who didn't feel it necessary to patronize the women they loved.

"I'd assume you're looking for me," she said, keeping her voice calm and detached. "How did you find me?"

"Your parents and I hired a private investigator. They thought you might have had a—a breakdown."

She bit back a laugh. "I'm mentally sound," she said. "I'm not crazy."

"The investigator tracked that Quinn fellow here after he figured out you'd left the station with him. He's spent the last few days following you. You've had quite a vacation. Or maybe we should call it a honeymoon?"

Payton glanced around. She and Brody had been so caught up in each other, they hadn't even noticed someone following them. "Why don't you just say what you came to say, Sam. I understand you're angry and I'm sorry for any embarrassment I caused. But you have to realize I saved us both a lot of heartache."

This seemed to soften his prickly facade. "Did you ever love me?"

"I think I did," she said, knowing it was probably a lie. "But I also think I was getting married to please my parents. They wanted me to be settled and happy and I never thought about what I really wanted."

"And this is it? Some guy you just met? I've read the report on him, Payton. Come on, you can't seriously be thinking of staying here with him. He's just some washed-up jock."

"I don't know what will happen tomorrow or the next day. But I'm happy right now, Sam. Happier than I've been in a long time."

"Payton, be practical. You don't belong here. You're thousands of miles from everything you know—your family and your friends. I forgive you. You made a mistake, but it's nothing that can't be fixed. We can begin again."

"I did make a mistake," she admitted. "I should have been honest about my feelings and my fears. I should have told you how I felt long before our wedding day."

"You got cold feet. Lots of women go through that. But give it a little more time and you'll realize who really loves you. And then you'll come home."

"Sam, I don't—"

He reached out and pressed his finger to her lips. "Don't. Just think about what I've said, Payton. I'm staying in Perth for the next three days. I think we should take some time to talk. To see if we can smooth out this wrinkle."

Wrinkle, Payton mused. She ran away from their wedding and took up with another man and Sam considered it a wrinkle. "I don't think we have anything to talk about."

"I'm at the Intercontinental. Room 1250. I'll be waiting for your call." With that, he turned and walked back to his car. Payton stared after him, wanting to shout out her anger. How dare he assume that she'd change her mind? She wasn't some feebleminded doormat who could be convinced by his mere appearance.

Sam could wait all he wanted, but she wasn't going to change her mind. She'd call her parents tonight and tell them exactly that. And then she'd tell them to talk some sense into her ex-fiancé. But first, she'd tell Brody about Sam's sudden appearance. Knowing Sam and his inability to accept losing at anything, she could expect another visit. She would not allow Brody to be caught off guard.

When she returned to Brody's apartment, she found him sitting on the sofa, examining his knee. He glanced up as she walked inside and she noticed the worried expression etched across his face.

"Is everything all right?" she asked. From the looks of things, now was not the time to bring up her ex-fiancé. That could wait until tomorrow, after the tryout.

"Sure," he said. He pushed to his feet and crossed to her, taking the bags from her hands. "Dinner?"

"Yes. I'm cooking something special. A good-luck meal. I figured it's about time to show you my true talents in the kitchen."

"You have talents in the kitchen too?" he teased, his mood shifting quickly. "I knew you were great in the bathroom, the bedroom and the living room. But the kitchen wasn't something I'd considered."

"I'm a very good cook," she explained.

He peered inside the bags, then pulled out the strawberries she'd purchased. Payton reached for them. "Those are for dessert," she said.

"Can't we have dessert first?" He took one from the bag and bit into it, then held it in front of her mouth.

Slowly, he drew the fruit across her lower lip. She ran her tongue over the sweet juice and smiled.

With a quick move, she bit down on the strawberry, then pulled him into a long, deep kiss. The taste of the berry exploded in her mouth, and Payton wasn't sure that she'd ever tasted something quite so wonderful.

The kiss went on forever, their hands moving over each other's body, so familiar yet still so exciting. He spanned her waist with his hands, then lifted her onto the granite countertop. The short shirt she wore bunched high on her thighs and he slipped his hand between her legs and began to caress her.

Payton knew his touch, yet every time he seduced her, he found a new way to take her to the heights of pleasure. He pushed her back until she was lying across the cool granite. Then he pulled her panties off and trailed kisses along the insides of her thighs.

She knew what was coming and waited, knowing the exquisite sensations his tongue could elicit. And then, he was there, sucking gently, making her writhe with the need for release.

She'd meant to tell him about Sam, but as her pleasure began to escalate, all thoughts of her former life dissolved. She was here with Brody now, and what they were doing was perfect. Nothing could possibly spoil it.

BRODY WINCED as he pushed up from a crouch and ran the width of the field. Though he was in pretty good shape, he hadn't really run full out since before his accident. When he reached the far side of the field, he gulped in a deep breath, then turned and ran back.

The scout scribbled something in his notebook, then nodded. "I understand your injury prevents lateral movement."

"Not prevents," Brody said. "Hampers. I'm just not as quick as I was. But it doesn't affect my kicking. You saw that. I put ten of them through the posts from fifty meters. I can do ten more. Hey, I can kick all day and I won't miss."

"But you'll have to run and tackle," he said. "And even though we have a rule against roughing the kicker, you will get knocked down. That knee isn't going to take much abuse."

"I know I can do this," Brody said. "Just give me a chance. I'll come to the States. I'll kick in your football stadium. I'll play for free."

The scout considered Brody's offer, then nodded his head. "You're a hell of a kicker. But I'm worried about the knee. The strength just isn't quite there. But you do some serious work and that might change. You should be running every day and doing some intense weight training. The NFL preseason starts the end of July. If a team is in need of a kicker, they'll be looking before the regular season begins in September." He held out his business card. "You call me after a month and we'll see where you're at."

Brody stared down at the card. "All right. I can do that. Thanks for taking the time."

"Good luck, son. I hope I hear from you."

Brody walked toward the exit, resigned to the fact that he'd given it his best try. Hell, he'd kicked well. No one could quarrel with that. But his knee wasn't what it should be. Even he knew it. He drew a deep breath, trying to push back the disappointment.

Though it wasn't good news, it wasn't really bad. He had a chance, if he put in a little work. He still had access to the team's training facilities and their physical therapists. Given a month, maybe he could gain more strength.

As he walked through the tunnel to the car park, he saw Payton standing in the entrance, her slender form outlined by the morning sun. She smiled and he felt his spirits rise. Even if the world was falling apart at his feet, she could still make him feel like a hero.

"How did it go?" she asked as he took her hand in his.

"I kicked well," he said. "But he didn't like the look of my knee."

"Well, you expected that," she said.

"He said I should work harder on rehab and then give him a call in a month."

"Are you going to do that?" she asked.

Brody shrugged. "I don't know. Maybe. It would give me more options." He smiled. "I can kick the damn ball. At least the next time one of their kickers goes down, he'll be thinking of me."

They drove back to his apartment, his mind distracted by the traffic. Every now and then, he caught Payton glancing over at him. He wanted to tell her how he was feeling—the frustration and the doubts—but his problems were his own. This afternoon, they'd find something to do that would take his mind off his troubles. And tomorrow, he'd figure out a plan.

As they drove up to the apartment, he reached out and took her hand. "Why don't we go surfing this afternoon." He looked over at her to see her gaze fixed on a car parked across the street from his building.

"What's wrong?"

"Keep driving," she said.

"Why? We need to get our gear if we're going surfing."

"Just keep going."

He did as he was told. After a few blocks, Brody drove in to an empty parking spot and pulled the truck out of gear. Then he turned to her. "Would you like to tell me what's going on?"

She gnawed at her lower lip, avoiding his eyes. "Yesterday, after I came back from the market, I saw Sam. My ex. He was parked in front of your apartment building waiting for me."

Brody felt as if he'd been hit in the gut. This didn't make sense. "You talked to Sam?"

She nodded, then risked a glance over at him. "I wanted to tell you yesterday, but you had the tryout today and I didn't want you to be upset. Besides, when I got home we got distracted and I guess I just forgot."

"You forgot?"

"Well, not exactly. It wasn't the right time."

"Which is it, Payton?"

She cursed softly. "What difference does it make? I'm telling you now. He asked if I'd come home. I told him no."

"Then what's he still doing here?"

"I guess he thinks I might change my mind."

Brody's fingers tightened on the steering wheel, his knuckles turning white. "And will you change your mind?"

"No," Payton insisted. "I don't want to marry him. I told him that. But he doesn't like to lose. And he certainly doesn't like to be embarrassed. He and my parents seem to think I've had some sort of mental breakdown and that if I just get a little help, I'll regain my senses."

"We're going back," Brody said. "I'll talk to the guy. I'll tell him to back off."

"No," Payton said. "This is my problem. I'll—"

"It's my problem now. He's screwing with *my* life."

"I know where he's staying. I'll call him tonight and tell him to go home. And I'll call my parents and let them know I'm going to stay in Australia for now."

Brody didn't like leaving it up to Payton. She'd obviously tried to convince Sam the first time they'd talked and it hadn't worked. Either Sam wasn't listening or she hadn't been forceful enough. But there would be no denying Brody's argument—either the guy would leave Fremantle immediately, or Brody would give him a thick ear.

"So what does this mean? We can't go back to the apartment?"

"Why don't we go get some lunch and maybe he'll be gone when we return." She reached out and pried his hand off the wheel, then laced her fingers through his. "As you've probably noticed, I'm not very good with confrontation."

"What are you talking about? You've told me off plenty of times."

"It's different with my family and with Sam. They make me feel—" Payton searched for the word "—small. They make me feel small."

He turned to look at her, noticing the uneasy expression on her face. Hell, he never wanted to do anything that made her feel that way. "You're one of the strongest, most determined people I know," he said. "Don't let them do that to you. Think of everything you've done over the past weeks."

Brody paused, carefully considering his next suggestion. He was tired of all the wondering—did she love him, would she stay, how did she really feel about Sam? There were too many unanswered questions that she had to settle once and for all. "I think you should go see him," Brody said.

"Really?"

"Why not? He was an important person in your life. Hell, you were going to marry him. Maybe he just needs some…what do they call that?"

"Closure?" she suggested.

"Right. Closure."

A long silence grew between them. "All right," she said softly. "If that's what you want, I'll go see him tomorrow."

It wasn't exactly what he wanted. But it was the quickest way to get to what he wanted. And for that, he was willing to take a risk. He'd give Sam Whitman one last chance to plead his case and if he didn't leave after that, Brody would personally escort him to the airport.

He wasn't about to let Payton go. At least, not without a good fight.

"WHAT DO YOU THINK?"

Brody frowned, staring down at the assortment of towels. He winced, then ran his hand through his hair. Payton could see the confusion in his eyes, but she suspected it had nothing to do with his choice of towels.

Payton had called Sam and agreed to meet him the

next morning. Since she'd made the decision, she and Brody hadn't spoken of it. In truth, she'd carefully avoided the subject. But she could see that it was killing Brody. He'd been hovering over her all day, obviously wanting to ask her what she would say, but afraid to bring up the subject.

"Ah…well, they're towels," he said. "I've never really had an opinion on towels. They're just sort of there when I need them." He nodded. "That's what I think."

"I mean the colors. Your bathroom is so neutral."

"Is it? What does that mean?"

He was going to make this difficult, Payton mused. She'd wondered if buying new towels for him was really a good idea. But she wanted to contribute something to the home they'd made together, even if it did mean spending a bit of his money. "Neutral means there's a lack of color."

"And color is good?"

"Yes. Now, do you like the ice blue or the burnt sienna? These are both masculine colors, but one is cool and the other is warm. I like the burnt sienna."

"Then I like that one, too. Don't I have towels?"

"Yes. But they're a little worn. And they're kind of mismatched. I just thought these would be pretty. And they're really soft. One hundred percent Egyptian cotton." He nodded mutely. Frustrated, Payton picked up the towels and shoved them back into the bag. "Never mind. I'll return them."

"No, no. Don't do that. I like them. I like the burnt sienna. And the blue, too. Maybe we could keep both. One color for summer and one for winter. Cool and warm, right?"

Payton gave him a grudging smile. "I just thought I could make your apartment look a little more homey."

"It doesn't look homey?"

She shook her head. "No. It looks like a bachelor's apartment. It's very nice, but very sterile. And if we're going to live here together, then I want it to be like a home."

A slow smile curled his lips. "A home. With me and you."

"Yes. I like it here."

"Is there anything else that needs fixing?" he asked.

"Well, the kitchen could use some nice towels. And a few accessories, maybe a bowl for the island, for fresh fruit. And some nice wineglasses to put in the china cabinet. Those refrigerator magnets have to go."

Brody chuckled softly. Then he dragged her into his arms, kissing her squarely on the mouth. "Do whatever you want," he said. "As long as you're staying, you can paint the place pink. And if you need more money, just ask."

She'd been thinking about exactly that subject. She wanted to contribute, to help pay for their living expenses. "I'm going to try to find a job," she said. "And to get a job, I suspect I'll need a work visa."

"We can think about that later. I have cash enough to last for a while."

"No, I want to contribute," she said.

"Then let's find out about a work visa." Brody reached out and removed the towels from the bag, stacking them up on the coffee table. "We'll go first thing tomorrow morning."

Payton forced a smile. "I'm going to see Sam

tomorrow morning. Remember?" She studied his expression. He didn't look happy. But then, he hadn't been very happy since Sam had appeared in Fremantle.

"We should go try out these towels," she said. "Let's take a shower."

Brody shook his head. "You think that if you seduce me, I'll stop worrying about him?"

"There's no need to worry," she assured him. "Brody, I'm decorating your apartment. I wouldn't do that unless I was planning to stay."

"He's leaving tomorrow?"

"That's what he said," Payton replied.

"Good. Then, day after, we can stop talking about him." He pushed her back on the sofa and crawled on top of her, rubbing his nose against hers. "Do you have a nice dress?"

"Not really."

"Then, go out and buy one. We're going out to a swank place tomorrow night for dinner. It's my birthday."

"It's your birthday? Why didn't you tell me?" Payton asked. "I'll make a cake. We'll have presents and a celebration."

"I just want to take my girl out," Brody said.

His girl. She liked the sound of that. It wasn't too serious. Yet, it did suggest a real relationship, one that was more than casual. "I'm not sure where to go to find something."

"There's a David Jones in the mall in Perth. It's the same store you went to in Brisbane."

"They have really pretty dresses there." She kissed him. "I'll go this afternoon. You can come and help me pick something out."

"Surprise me," he said. Brody brushed the hair out of her eyes. "When is your birthday?"

"August tenth," she said. "I was born twelve minutes before midnight."

Payton realized they didn't know the little details about each other's lives. Maybe it was time to find out. "What's your favorite color?" she asked.

"Neutral," he teased. "No, it was blue. But now, it's this really pretty shade of pink." Brody smiled. "Exactly the color of your lips."

Payton groaned inwardly. Her attempt to learn more about him was swiftly turning into a full-out seduction. But then, they had plenty of time to go over the silly little details. "What is your favorite sexual fantasy?" she asked.

He laughed sharply. "How did we go from colors to sexual fantasies?"

Payton shrugged. "Just curious."

He thought about his answer for a long time, then smiled. "There is this one. I'm asleep and I'm having this dream that there's a woman in bed with me. And she's doing all kinds of wonderful things with her lips and her tongue. And I open my eyes and it's not a dream."

"Has it ever happened before?" Payton asked.

"No," he said.

"Your birthday is coming up. That could be arranged, you know."

"Arranged? Only if you're the woman I'm waking up to. I'd reckon that would be a bonzer prezzy."

"Bonzer is good?"

"Very good. Great. Incredible. The best."

"Hmm. That's a lot to live up to. Maybe I should just buy you a bonzer watch. Or a bonzer shirt."

"Do not tease me," he said. "It's my birthday. And as my girl, it's your job to treat me special."

Payton giggled. "It's not your birthday yet." Now that she'd decided to stay, she had every intention of making all Brody's fantasies come true. Life—and sex—with Brody would be one long adventure.

9

THE BUZZER ON the security system startled Brody. Payton had left less than an hour ago to shop for a dress for tomorrow's birthday celebration. He hadn't expected her to return until just before dinner.

He pushed the button and leaned in. "Did you forget your key?"

There was a long pause on the other end. "I'm looking for Brody Quinn."

"And who might you be?" Brody asked.

"Sam. Sam Whitman."

Brody stepped back from the intercom, then cursed softly. What the hell was this? Payton had assured him that she'd called Sam and told him she would see him in the morning. Either he was a very impatient man or he wanted to talk to Brody directly.

Brody drew a deep breath. "She's not here," he said.

"I'm here to talk to you," Sam said. "Man to man."

Brody shook his head, then opened the front door and walked to the lift. If this guy wanted to talk, they'd talk. But Brody was going to have much more to say than "get the hell out of our lives." As he rode the lift down to the lobby, he carefully schooled his temper. The last thing he wanted to do was punch the guy. There was no need to get physical. But he was prepared to take it that far if the situation warranted.

He'd seen the photo of Sam on the Internet and knew what to expect. But when he walked into the lobby, Brody was surprised at how slight he was. In a bar brawl, Sam Whitman wouldn't last a minute.

To Brody's delight, Whitman seemed to be a bit intimidated by Brody's size. Brody had at least ten centimeters on him and a good fifteen kilos. "What do you want?" he demanded.

"I have some things to say about Payton."

"She plans to stay here with me. She was going to stop by your hotel tomorrow morning and let you know."

Sam paused, as if considering his next comment carefully. "You don't find it unusual that she'd abandon her family and friends? Without a second thought?"

"No," Brody lied. "Not after the way you treated her. She has a right to make her own decisions."

"I think we both have to be honest," Sam said. "Maybe I didn't give her the attention she needed. And I'll admit, I might have focused on work too much. But I can give her a very comfortable life. From what I know of you, you can't."

Brody quelled a surge of temper. He knew it was the only advantage that Sam Whitman had on him. And Whitman obviously wasn't afraid to use it.

"I have some opportunities," Brody said. "Besides, we can always live on the station with my family. Payton loves it there."

"For how long?" Sam asked. "How long until the novelty wears off and she grows tired of being isolated from everything she knows and loves?"

He was saying the same things Brody had said to himself. "Do you honestly think you can buy her back?"

"No. But I believe if you really love her, you'll consider what's best for her. I believe if you're selfish enough to keep her here, you'll pay the price later. And by isolating her from her family and friends, you're allowing her to avoid the consequences of her actions." Sam reached into his jacket pocket and pulled out a leather wallet, then withdrew an envelope from it. "This is an airline ticket and enough cash to get her home."

"What makes you think I'll give this to her?"

"Because you want to know as much as I do," Sam said. "You love her enough not to leave any stone unturned. Send her home. If she comes back to you, you'll know she's made her choice." He held out his hand. "May the best man win."

Brody bit back a curse. This guy was arrogant and condescending and in need of a good beat-down. But he was also right. If Brody did want to keep Payton in his life permanently, then she'd have to face up to her past mistakes. It was better to lose her now than later.

He reached out and shook Sam's hand, then nodded. "She loves me," he said.

"Then I guess you have nothing to worry about. Tell her good-bye. And I'll see her back home."

With that, Sam turned on his heel and walked out of the lobby. He watched as Sam jogged across the street and got into his car. Then Brody glanced down at the airline ticket. He ought to just toss it in the rubbish and forget it ever existed.

Why not? He could accept the risk that it would all explode in his face at some point. He'd have more time to convince Payton she'd made the best choice by staying. But Sam was right on one point. It was probably better to know how she really felt, before investing his heart in a relationship that was doomed from the start.

Brody walked back to the lift and pushed the button, then stepped inside after the doors opened. A single shot at an NFL career wasn't enough. If he wanted to compete with Sam Whitman's millions, he had to look at other options.

The moment he got back to his apartment, Brody found his phone and dialed the Dockers' office. When the receptionist answered, Brody asked to speak to John Cook. When the assistant coach got on the line, Brody drew a deep breath and said a silent prayer.

"John. Brody Quinn here. Say, I was wondering if you still had the name of that bloke at Seven Network. You know, the one you thought might be able to find a spot for me as an analyst?"

To Brody's surprise, Cook had the number at hand and encouraged Brody to make the call. They chatted for a few minutes about Brody's knee and the possibility of surgery, but Brody cut the conversation short and hung up. After a half hour, he had a list of seven contacts for a wide range of jobs, from school coach to equipment salesman.

He stared at the phone for a long time, trying to put his thoughts in order. Then he tossed the phone on the sofa and stood up. This was far too important to bungle. The NFL would pay the best, but television was more secure. He'd follow Callum's advice and write everything down first, the pros and cons of all his options.

Brody found a pad of paper, sat down at the table and carefully wrote out the skills that he possessed. He'd always been the club's best student of the game. He read the opposition like no other player and could talk at length about a player's strengths and weaknesses. He had a good mind for statistics and remembered almost everything he read. He didn't stammer or mumble and his teammates had often teased him about his pretty face. And he was considered quite charming.

"What more is there?" Brody asked himself, staring at the list. He owned a suit and tie and a decent pair of shoes. He wrote that down, though he assumed if he got a job in the business world, he'd need a better wardrobe. He started a list for the NFL job and even made one for getting back into Aussie football.

Brody heard the front door open and turned to see Payton walking in. Their eyes met and for a moment, Brody forgot to breathe. He still found himself amazed that she'd wandered into his life. How the hell had he gotten so lucky?

"You're home early," he said, glancing over at the plane ticket he'd left on the table.

She held up a sheaf of papers. "I stopped by the immigration office on my way back from shopping. I have to fill out all this paperwork and then call back for an appointment." Payton dropped her shopping bags on the floor, then sat down on his lap and slipped her arms around his neck. "What happens if they don't let me stay? What if they force me to go home?"

"Maybe you need to go home," he said. The moment the words slipped out of his mouth, he wanted to take them back. Why would he encourage her to leave? Was he compelled to test her feelings for him? Brody took the plane ticket from the table and held it out to her.

"What's that?"

"A ticket home," he said. "Sam dropped by. I guess he got tired of waiting for you and decided to talk to me."

Her expression turned angry. "I left a message that I was coming to see him tomorrow. He always has to control everything. God, I hate that about him. I'm not going home. And I'm not going to talk to him again. I'll just return the ticket. Or better yet, exchange it for tickets we can use together."

"I think you should go home. Payton, I don't want to constantly be looking over my shoulder, waiting for him to turn up again like he did today. You need to clean up the mess you left behind and then, if you still want to, come back. But this is always going to be hanging between us, Payton. I'm always going to wonder if I'll wake up someday and you'll be gone."

She bit on her lower lip, her eyes filling with tears. "So you want me to leave?"

"Of course not. But if you're going to stay, I want you to stay forever. And if you don't smooth things out with your family, you're always going to regret that. Do it now. Make amends. And then come home to me."

A long silence grew between them as she considered his suggestion. "You're right," she finally said. "This whole thing has been hanging over us like a dark cloud. I know what I want and I shouldn't be afraid to tell them." Payton cupped his face in her hands and stared into his eyes. "I'll go back day after tomorrow," she said. "After we've celebrated your birthday. And I'll call my parents and let them know I'm coming home." Payton leaned forward and gave him a fierce kiss. "I will come back. You can count on it."

Brody's pulse leaped. He cupped her face in his hands and molded her mouth to his. How would he live without this? After a day or two, he'd be ready to hop a flight to the States and drag her back.

But he'd have to be strong and hope that she would return and stay for good. Brody slipped his arm beneath her knees and stood, then slowly walked toward the bedroom, their mouths still caught in a deep kiss.

As he lowered her onto his bed, they broke apart for a moment. He stared down into her beautiful face and tried to memorize all the tiny details that he'd begun to take for granted. He didn't even have a photo of her. But then, perhaps that was for the best.

He could believe she'd existed in a dream, that what they'd shared hadn't been real. If she didn't return, he'd continue with the fantasy. And if she did, reality would be better than anything he could have ever imagined.

They undressed each other slowly, taking the time to touch each inch of exposed skin. There were so many spots on her body he'd lingered over, spots made just for his lips or his tongue or his touch. In his eyes, she was perfection and there would never be another woman like her.

And when they finally came together in a long, delicious possession, he was already regretting what he'd done. He should have burned the ticket, should have trusted his instincts and kept her with him.

He thrust deep and held her close, desperate to seal the bond they shared. Again and again, they moved together and when their release finally came, Brody knew just one thing was certain. He loved Payton and if giving her up meant assuring her happiness, he'd do it in a heartbeat.

JFK WAS CROWDED with summer tourists, the concourse a maze of luggage and late passengers. Her flight from Perth had been a marathon affair, though passed in the comfort of first class. She'd boarded a Qantas flight almost thirty-five hours ago and had changed planes in Melbourne and Los Angeles. At this point, she could barely summon the energy to lift her bag onto her shoulder, much less marshal the resolve to face her parents.

But her trip was far from over. Before she'd left Perth, she'd booked her return flight and a night at an airport hotel, putting the charges on her credit card. One last thing her father would pay for before she was completely on her own. She was due to get right back on the plane in another twenty-four hours. In all, she'd be apart from Brody for three and a half days—enough time to realize she could never stay away longer.

They'd had a wonderful birthday celebration, though it was laced with the bittersweet knowledge that they'd soon be miles apart. After returning from the restaurant, they'd stripped out of their fancy clothes and made love all night long.

When it was time for her to leave, he'd reluctantly let her go. He'd decided to call a cab, rather than drive her to the airport himself, and Payton was glad for it. Emotional goodbyes would have been too difficult to handle. She was determined to get her problems solved and then return. Neither one of them would have time to be sad.

Payton wondered why she'd even bothered to leave. She didn't need to see Sam again. As for her parents, she could have invited them to Fremantle for a visit and a chance to meet the man she loved.

Payton stopped short, causing a traffic problem on the concourse. She hadn't admitted it to herself until now, but she was in love with Brody. It had taken thirty-five hours in and out of the air for her to come to that realization, but at least she was dead certain of it. She loved Brody Quinn and deep down inside, she knew he loved her, as well.

"So what am I doing here?" she muttered, staring at her surroundings. Payton hoisted her bag back up on her shoulder and started off again. "Closure," she murmured.

How wonderful would it be to return to Brody without a single thing hanging over their heads? She smiled to herself as she walked, thinking about the last time she'd seen him. He'd stood in the doorway of his apartment building, watching her get into the cab. He'd looked so sad, almost as if he didn't believe he'd ever see her again. She'd prove him wrong.

Her parents had promised to meet her outside the security checkpoint and as she neared the spot, Payton said a silent prayer that they'd kept their promise. As she worked her way through the crowd, she caught sight of Sam. He waved at her and she started toward him. He met her halfway, then grabbed her bag.

"I thought my parents would meet me."

"They're waiting in the Red Carpet Club just down the concourse. I wanted to talk to you first."

"I don't have anything to say to you, Sam."

"I have something to say to you," he said. He took her elbow and steered her over to a row of chairs set against the wall. "Sit."

Payton gave him a withering look. She wouldn't be ordered around like some naughty pet.

"Please, sit down," Sam amended, motioning to the chair. "I have something I need to tell you before you talk to your parents."

She frowned, taking in the stricken expression on Sam's face. Payton had never seen him so worried. Her stomach lurched. "What is it? Are my parents all right? Has something happened? Did someone die?"

"No," Sam said. He sat down, then pulled her down beside him. "It's me."

"You're dying?" Payton asked.

A wry smile touched his lips. "Metaphorically, yes." Sam drew a deep breath, then met her gaze. "For the past three years, I've been carrying on an affair with my executive assistant. Your father found out about it and I'm sure your parents will bring it up. They think that's why you ran out on the wedding."

Payton stared at him, his words a jumble in her mind. "You were having an affair? You were cheating on me? And my father knew about it?"

"Yes. To all three questions. I know how you must feel and I can only beg for your forgiveness and spend the rest of my life making this up to you. It's over. It's been over for a month now and—"

"Wait," Payton said, holding up her hand. "A month? You mean, it was still going on while we were in—" She stopped, stunned by the realization. "She was there. In Fiji. Emily was there. We invited her to our wedding. Oh, my God. You were planning to carry on after we were married?"

"I know this must be a shock, but I can assure you that—"

Payton shook her head, a laugh bubbling up inside her. "I knew something was wrong. I trusted my instincts and I was right." She stood and picked up her bag from the floor, slinging it over her shoulder. "Do you want to know what I feel, Sam?" She shrugged. "Nothing. I feel nothing. I thought I loved you, but I know now that what we had wasn't love. It was obligation. And I'm fine with this."

He jumped up and reached for her arm, but Payton avoided his grasp. "Unfortunately, you won't be taking over Daddy's bank, but I'm sure you'll find comfort in the fact that you can keep sleeping with Emily." Payton held out her hand. "Goodbye, Sam. Have a nice life."

He took her hand and gave it a weak shake. Then, Payton turned on her heel and headed down the concourse. As she walked, she tried to make sense of what Sam had told her. Her parents had known about his affair and they'd still gone ahead with the wedding plans. How was that possible?

When she reached the first-class lounge, she stood in the doorway, her gaze falling on the handsome couple sitting at a nearby table. They spotted her at the same time and her mother rushed up to her, arms thrown open. She gathered Payton in a frantic embrace, hugging her tightly. "You're home," she cried. "Thank God. I was beginning to wonder if I'd ever see you again."

A moment later, her father appeared at her side and patted her on the shoulder. "There, there. Well, I'm happy to see you've come to your senses, Payton. Come on, let's get out of here. We have a car waiting."

"No," Payton said.

Her father arched his brow. "No? How do you propose we get home?"

Payton straightened her spine and took a deep breath. "I'm not going home, Daddy. Not tonight."

Her mother gave Payton's arm a gentle squeeze. "Oh, George. She's going to Sam's, of course. Darling, we couldn't be happier. You know how much we adore Sam. And he loves you. Just wait, this whole terrible embarrassment will be forgotten in no time."

"Mother, I'm not going to Sam's." She took her mother's hand and pulled her along with her toward their table. "I think we should order some wine, sit down and talk. I have something I need to tell you."

"She's pregnant." Her mother pressed a hand to her heart and closed her eyes. Her father held her elbow to keep her upright.

"I'm not pregnant!" Payton groaned. "Why would you think that?"

"Sam said you were—oh, how did he say it, George?"

"Shacked up, Margie," her father said. "He said Payton was shacked up with some unemployed soccer player."

"Football," Payton said. "Aussie rules football. Mother, Father, sit down," she ordered. It was time they started treating her like an adult and not some eager child always willing to please. This conversation would be between three reasonable adults—or one reasonable adult trying to calm two irrational-overbearing adults. She drew a steadying breath. "I'll be right back."

She strode up to the bar, ordered three glasses of Merlot and paid with one of the twenties that Sam had given her. Then she carried the wine to the table and sat down.

"Why are we staying here?" her mother asked. "Why don't we go home and have a drink? I'm sure the quality of this wine isn't up to the standards of what we have in our wine cellar." She took a sip and wrinkled her nose. "Just as I suspected."

"This is ridiculous." Her father pushed away from the table. "You're coming home with us right now, Payton. You are going to get a good night's sleep and then we are going to figure out how you can make this all up to Sam."

She shook her head. "I don't love him. And neither should you. He cheated on me. You knew and you were going to let me marry him all the same. You two spent a lifetime trying to protect me and then, when I really needed you the most, you were ready to walk away, to let me marry a man who didn't love me."

"Sam assured me the affair was over," her father said. "And that it wouldn't happen again."

"Well, he wasn't telling you the truth. Thank God, I figured it out."

"When did you find out?" her mother asked.

"A few minutes ago," Payton said. "But I knew something was wrong for a long time. I felt it in the weeks before the wedding. And in Fiji. That's why I ran." An image of Brody flashed in her mind and she smiled. "And I'm lucky I did. Because I've met a man I can really love and trust, a man who wants me and not the bank I'll inherit. I have to live my life now on my own. And I'm going to do that in Australia. With Brody."

"What is she saying, George?" her mother asked.

"She's just distraught. You need help," her father

said, turning to Payton. "We can get you help. A nice quiet place to get some perspective."

Payton giggled softly. "Daddy, I don't need help. I'm perfectly sane and I'm happier than I've ever been. And I hope someday you'll come to visit me. I'd love for you to meet Brody. He's a wonderful man. Or maybe, we'll come here for a visit. Brody might have a tryout with a football team later this summer." She gulped down the rest of her wine, then stood, satisfied that she'd said everything that needed saying.

Though she ought to have been angrier over her parents' deception, there wasn't really a point. Every-thing they'd done had led to Brody and that was all that mattered. She rounded the table and kissed them both on the cheek. "I have to go now. I think I might be able to catch the flight back tonight if I hurry."

"You only just got here," her father said.

"And now I have to go," Payton replied, picking up her bag. "I love you both. And don't worry, I know exactly what I'm doing."

She walked to the doorway of the bar, then turned and waved at her stunned parents. It was enough for them to see that she was healthy and happy. They'd get over her broken engagement and their disappointment that Sam wouldn't be a part of the family. And they'd find a way to explain the embarrassment of the wedding. And maybe someday they would meet Brody and understand why she loved him.

As much as she wanted to feel regret while walking away from them, Payton couldn't. She was returning to the man she loved, to a land she was learning to love and to a life that would be built on love. She

wasn't frightened or nervous or anything but bliss-
fully happy.

She checked the signs at the end of the concourse and
headed toward the Qantas desk. If she hurried, she could
hop the 7:10 flight to Australia, a full day before her
scheduled return. Then, in about thirty hours, she'd be
back in Brody's life—and in his arms—for good.

"DAVEY, GRAB ME that spanner." Brody crawled halfway
down the windmill and waited as the kid searched the
ground at his feet. "Next to my saddlebags."

He picked up a tool. "This one?"

"No, the big one."

Davey finally found the tool, then climbed up the
ladder and handed it to Brody. They'd been working
together all day, greasing and adjusting the six windmills
close to the station. Tomorrow they'd catch the ones on
the outlying pastures, traveling by ATV rather than horse.

Brody had decided to return to the station after just
one day alone in Fremantle. The apartment seemed so
empty without Payton there and he found himself
spending every waking minute thinking about her. He
could rehab his knee as easily on the station as he could
in Fremantle, and he'd have work to occupy his mind
the rest of the day. Station work was difficult and exhausting—and exactly what he needed.

He wasn't sure when Payton would return. She'd
promised to call once everything had been settled, but
he expected she'd spend at least a week or two in the
States before she left again. He'd decided to go on as if
she wasn't going to return. Then, everything after that—
if there was anything—would be like a gift.

Brody climbed back up to the top of the windmill, the spanner tucked into his jacket pocket and the grease gun still clutched in his hand. As he went through the maintenance routine, he heard the sound of a plane overhead and glanced up to see Teague coming in from the east.

He hadn't seen Teague at all since his return and Callum had ridden out an hour after Gemma had left a day ago, heading into the outback with his horse, his pack and his rifle. He'd left Skip in charge of preparations for the mustering, a sure sign that he was upset. Now that Teague was back, Brody would get some answers. He had tried not to dwell on his brothers' love lives. Thinking about their happiness only made his life seem emptier.

"What is he doing?" Davey asked.

Brody glanced over his shoulder to see Teague circling the plane. "I don't know." He watched as Teague made a wide sweep around the windmill, wiggling his wings before he headed toward the airstrip.

Brody finished his work, then carefully surveyed the landscape from his perch high above the ground. He used to love this view when he was a kid. He always thought if he just looked hard enough, he could see the real world in the distance. Now he took some comfort in the fact that he was isolated from that world.

If things didn't work out the way he'd planned, then he'd return to the station for good and make his life here in Queensland. He'd always have a place with his brothers and there was some comfort in that.

"Are we done?" Davey called.

"Yeah," Brody replied. "Pack it up. It's getting late. We should start back if we want to make it by dinner."

Davey gathered the tools, then strapped the pouch to his horse. By the time Brody joined him, Davey was mounted and ready to ride. There was no keeping him from a meal. Davey kicked his horse into a gallop, but Brody decided to take a slower pace.

"Come on," Davey shouted over his shoulder, pulling his horse up to wait.

"Go ahead," Brody called. "I want to enjoy the ride."

"Suit yourself. But Mary's got pork chops tonight. If you don't sit down on time, the rest of the boys will eat all the potatoes."

He waved Davey off and watched as the kid took off in a cloud of dust. Brody wasn't anxious to get back to the dinner table. Since he'd returned, he'd been grabbing a plate and eating by himself, too preoccupied to socialize. Mary and the jackaroos had given him a wide berth and he'd been grateful for it.

As he rode toward the house, he noticed the Fraser shack in the distance. His mind wandered back to the night he'd spent there with Payton. Everything had been so new with them then, so exciting. Only a few weeks had passed since, but it seemed like a lifetime.

He wondered what Payton was doing, trying to calculate the time difference between New York and Queensland. There was almost a twelve-hour difference, so it was the middle of the night there. Was she sleeping alone or had Sam convinced her to return to his bed?

Brody cursed beneath his breath, brushing the image from his mind. He wanted to believe that thoughts of him filled her mind, that she missed what they had together, that she ached for him the way he ached for her. Sleep hadn't come easily since she'd gone.

He fixed his gaze on the horizon and let the horse navigate. It felt good to think about her, to rewind every encounter and enjoy them all over again. They'd been wonderful together, both in and out of bed. He closed his eyes and tipped his face up, the sun warm on his back, exhaustion setting in.

Maybe he'd sleep tonight, he mused. Perhaps his bed wouldn't seem so cold and empty. It had to happen sooner or later. The loneliness would fade and he'd get his life back—pitiful as it was.

When he opened his eyes again, he noticed a rider approaching from the direction of the homestead. He squinted to see in the late-afternoon light, trying to make out who it was. Slowly, he realized it was a woman. Hayley?

Suddenly, the rider pulled to a stop and jumped off the horse. Brody's breath caught in his chest. He blinked hard, wondering if he was imagining her, like a mirage in the middle of the desert. He kicked his horse into a trot and covered the distance between them.

As he approached, she pulled off her stockman's hat and her curly hair fell down around her shoulders. Brody smiled. If this was a dream, then he planned to enjoy it.

He reined in his horse before he reached her, then slid down to stand beside it. For a long time, they stood facing each other, neither one of them moving. And then, at the very same moment, they covered the distance between them in just a few seconds.

Payton launched herself into his arms and he picked her up and spun her around. She felt real, warm and soft, the scent of her hair filling his head. "Is it really you?"

"I think so," Payton said. "I can't have changed that much in four days."

He set her down and stepped back to look into her eyes. "You're more beautiful, I think. Is that possible?" Brody took her face in his hands and kissed her, his tongue delving into her mouth and savoring her taste. "Did you even go home?"

Payton nodded. "I did. I saw Sam and my parents and I turned around and came back. When I got to New York, I realized it was the last place in the world I wanted to be. You shouldn't have made me leave, but I'm glad I put that part of my life to rest."

"I won't do that again," Brody said. "God, I missed you. How did you get here?"

"Teague picked me up. When I got to Fremantle and you weren't there, I figured you might have come back to the station. I flew to Brisbane and then called Teague and he came to get me. I thought it might be nice to surprise you."

"Nice," he said. "I like *nice* now. Coming back to me is definitely nice."

"I may have to leave again if they don't extend my visa. But maybe, we can go to New York for a visit."

"Or for that football tryout. I'm going to give that a go. And if it doesn't work out, I have some other interesting prospects."

She pushed up onto her toes and kissed him softly. "I don't care what you do or where we live. I don't ever want to be away from you again. I—I think I might love you."

Brody chuckled softly. For now, he was happy with a vague statement of love. He could wait for her feelings to grow stronger. "I think I might love you, too. A lot."

He grabbed her hand, then pulled it to his lips. "So, what are we going to do with ourselves?"

"Mary's making dinner. We could eat and then go for a swim."

"Aren't you tired? You've been on a plane for the better part of four days."

"About seventy hours," she said. "I've taken off and landed sixteen times."

"Then I definitely think you need to get to bed. Right now. For your own health. And mine." He glanced over his shoulder. "We could head over to the shack and spend the night there."

"But we're not lost. And that would be trespassing."

Brody smoothed his thumb over her lower lip. "This all started with a life of crime. I think we can live dangerously."

Payton threw her arms around his neck. "Forget about nice. I'm really starting to enjoy dangerous."

He wrapped his hands around her waist and set her back on her horse, then remounted. As they rode toward the sunset, Brody wondered at how his life had changed so much in such a short time. There were no answers to his questions, and maybe there never would be. But Payton was here, with him, from half a world away.

This hadn't been his dream, but it was now. And it was better than any dream he could have ever imagined for himself.

* * * * *

One Quinn down, two to go.
Which will be the next to fall?
Find out next month!

*Celebrate 60 years of pure
reading pleasure with Harlequin®!*

*Harlequin Presents® is proud to introduce
its gripping new miniseries,*
THE ROYAL HOUSE OF KAREDES.
*An exquisite coronation diamond, split
as a symbol of a warring royal family's feud,
is missing! But whoever reunites the
diamond halves will rule all….*

*Welcome to eight brand-new titles that unfold
to reveal the stories of kings and queens,
princes and princesses torn apart by pride
and power, but finally reunited by love.*

Step into the world of Karedes with
BILLIONAIRE PRINCE, PREGNANT MISTRESS
*Available July 2009
from Harlequin Presents®.*

ALEXANDROS KAREDES, SNOW DUSTING the shoulders of his leather jacket and glittering like jewels in his dark hair, stood at the door. Maria felt the blood drain from her head.

"Good evening, Ms. Santos."

His voice was as she remembered it. Deep. Husky. Perfect English, but with the faintest hint of a Greek accent. And cold, as cold as it had been that awful morning she would never forget, when he'd accused her of horrible things, called her terrible names....

"Aren't you going to ask me in?"

She fought for composure. Last time they'd faced each other, they'd been on his turf. Now they were on hers. She was in command here, and that meant everything.

"There's a sign on the door downstairs," she said, her tone every bit as frigid as his. "It says, 'No soliciting or vagrants.'"

His lips drew back in a wolfish grin. "Very amusing."

"What do you want, Prince Alexandros?"

A tight smile eased across his mouth and it killed her that even now, knowing he was a vicious, arrogant man, she couldn't help but notice what a handsome mouth it was. Chiseled. Generous. Beautiful, like the rest of him, which made him living proof that beauty could, indeed, be only skin deep.

"Such formality, Maria. You were hardly so proper the last time we were together."

She knew his choice of words was deliberate. She felt her face heat; she couldn't help that but she damned well didn't have to let him lure her into a verbal sparring match.

"I'll ask you once more, your highness. What do you want?"

"Ask me in and I'll tell you."

"I have no intention of asking you in. Tell me why you're here or don't. It's your choice, just as it will be my choice to shut the door in your face."

He laughed. It infuriated her but she could hardly blame him. He was tall—six two, six three—and though he stood with one shoulder leaning against the door frame, hands tucked casually into the pockets of the jacket, his pose was deceptive. He was strong, with the leanly muscled body of a well-trained athlete.

She remembered his body with painful clarity. The feel of him under her hands. The power of him moving over her. The taste of him on her tongue.

Suddenly, he straightened, his laughter gone. "I have not come this distance to stand in your doorway," he said coldly, "and I am not going to leave until I am ready to do so. I suggest you stand aside and stop behaving like a petulant child."

A petulant child? Was that what he thought? This man who had spent hours making love to her and had then accused her of—of trading her body for profit?

Except it had not been love, it had been sex. And the sooner she got rid of him, the better.

She let go of the doorknob and stepped aside. "You have five minutes."

He strolled past her, bringing cold air and the scent of the night with him. She swung toward him, arms folded. He reached past her, pushed the door closed, then folded his arms, too. She wanted to open the door again but she'd be damned if she was going to get into a who's-in-charge-here argument with him. She was in charge, and he would surely see a tussle over the ground rules as a sign of weakness.

Instead, she looked past him at the big clock above her work table.

"Ten seconds gone," she said briskly. "You're wasting time, your highness."

"What I have to say will take longer than five minutes."

"Then you'll just have to learn to economize. More than five minutes, I'll call the police."

Instantly, his hand was wrapped around her wrist. He tugged her toward him, his dark-chocolate eyes almost black with anger.

"You do that and I'll tell every tabloid shark I can contact about how Maria Santos tried to buy a five-hundred-thousand-dollar commission by seducing a prince." He smiled thinly. "They'll lap it up."

* * * * *

*What will it take for this billionaire prince to
realize he's falling in love with his mistress…?*
Look for
BILLIONAIRE PRINCE, PREGNANT MISTRESS
by Sandra Marton
Available July 2009
from Harlequin Presents®.

We'll be spotlighting a different series every month throughout 2009 to celebrate our 60th anniversary.

Look for Harlequin® Presents in July!

TWO CROWNS, TWO ISLANDS, ONE LEGACY
A royal family, torn apart by pride and its lust for power, reunited by purity and passion

Step into the world of Karedes beginning this July with

BILLIONAIRE PRINCE, PREGNANT MISTRESS
by
Sandra Marton

Eight volumes to collect and treasure!

REQUEST YOUR FREE BOOKS!

2 FREE NOVELS PLUS 2 FREE GIFTS!

HARLEQUIN®

Blaze™

Red-hot reads!

YES! Please send me 2 FREE Harlequin® Blaze™ novels and my 2 FREE gifts (gifts are worth about $10). After receiving them, if I don't wish to receive any more books, I can return the shipping statement marked "cancel". If I don't cancel, I will receive 6 brand-new novels every month and be billed just $4.24 per book in the U.S. or $4.71 per book in Canada. That's a savings of 15% off the cover price. It's quite a bargain. Shipping and handling is just 50¢ per book.* I understand that accepting the 2 free books and gifts places me under no obligation to buy anything. I can always return a shipment and cancel at any time. Even if I never buy another book, the two free books and gifts are mine to keep forever.

151 HDN EYS2   351 HDN EYTE

Name	(PLEASE PRINT)	
Address		Apt. #
City	State/Prov.	Zip/Postal Code

Signature (if under 18, a parent or guardian must sign)

Mail to the **Harlequin Reader Service:**
IN U.S.A.: P.O. Box 1867, Buffalo, NY 14240-1867
IN CANADA: P.O. Box 609, Fort Erie, Ontario L2A 5X3

Not valid to current subscribers of Harlequin Blaze books.

Want to try two free books from another line?
Call 1-800-873-8635 or visit www.morefreebooks.com.

* Terms and prices subject to change without notice. Prices do not include applicable taxes. N.Y. residents add applicable sales tax. Canadian residents will be charged applicable provincial taxes and GST. Offer not valid in Quebec. This offer is limited to one order per household. All orders subject to approval. Credit or debit balances in a customer's account(s) may be offset by any other outstanding balance owed by or to the customer. Please allow 4 to 6 weeks for delivery. Offer available while quantities last.

Your Privacy: Harlequin Books is committed to protecting your privacy. Our Privacy Policy is available online at www.eHarlequin.com or upon request from the Reader Service. From time to time we make our lists of customers available to reputable third parties who may have a product or service of interest to you. If you would prefer we not share your name and address, please check here. ☐

HB09R3

In 2009 Harlequin celebrates
60 years of pure reading pleasure!

We're marking this occasion by offering
16 **FREE** full books to download and read.

Visit

www.HarlequinCelebrates.com

to choose from a variety of
great romance stories
that are absolutely **FREE!**

(Total approximate retail value of $60)

We invite you to visit and share the Web site
with your friends, family
and anyone who enjoys reading.

You're invited to join our Tell Harlequin Reader Panel!

By joining our new reader panel you will:

- Receive Harlequin® books—they are FREE and yours to keep with no obligation to purchase anything!
- Participate in fun online surveys
- Exchange opinions and ideas with women just like you
- Have a say in our new book ideas and help us publish the best in women's fiction

In addition, you will have a chance to win great prizes and receive special gifts! See Web site for details. Some conditions apply. Space is limited.

To join, visit us at

www.TellHarlequin.com.

Do you crave dark and sensual paranormal tales?

Get your fix with Silhouette Nocturne!

In print:
Two new titles available every month wherever books are sold.

Online:
Nocturne eBooks available monthly from **www.silhouettenocturne.com**.

Nocturne Bites:
Short sensual paranormal stories available monthly online from **www.nocturnebites.com** and in print with the Nocturne Bites collections available April 2009 and October 2009 wherever books are sold.

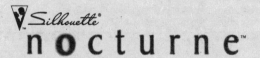

www.silhouettenocturne.com
www.paranormalromanceblog.com

HARLEQUIN *Blaze*

COMING NEXT MONTH
Available June 30, 2009

#477 ENDLESS SUMMER Julie Kenner, Karen Anders, Jill Monroe
Three surfer chicks + three hot guys = one endless summer. The Maui beaches will never be the same after these couples hit the waves and live their sexiest dreams to the fullest!

#478 HARD TO RESIST Samantha Hunter
American Heroes
Sexy, straight-as-an-arrow Texas Ranger Jarod Wyatt is awestruck by the New York skyline and the stunning photographer snapping his portrait. As soon as Lacey Graham spies the hunk through her lens she knows she has to have him…even if she has to commit a crime to get the good cop's attention!

#479 MAKE ME YOURS Betina Krahn
Blaze Historicals
Mariah Eller was only trying to save her inn from being trashed. So how did she manage to attract the unwanted—and erotic—attention of the Prince of Wales? Not that being desired by royalty is bad—except Mariah much prefers Jack St. Lawrence, the prince's sexy best friend….

#480 TWIN SEDUCTION Cara Summers
The Wrong Bed: Again and Again
Jordan Ware is in over her head. According to her late mother's will, she has to trade places with a twin sister she didn't know she had. She thinks it will be tricky, but possible…until she finds herself in bed with her twin's fiancé.

#481 THE SOLDIER Rhonda Nelson
Uniformly Hot!
Army Ranger Adam McPherson is back home, thanks to a roadside bomb that cost him part of his leg. But he's not out yet. He's been offered a position in the Special Forces once he's back on his feet. The problem? His childhood nemesis seems determined to keep him off his feet—and in her bed….

#482 THE MIGHTY QUINNS: TEAGUE Kate Hoffmann
Quinns Down Under
Romeo and Juliet, Outback-style. Teague Quinn has loved Haley Fraser since they were both kids. But time and feuding families got in the way. Now Teague and Haley are both back home—and back in bed! Can they make first love last the second time around?